THE CURIOUS CLICHE OF THE BLACK SCARAB

(THE DRY CRUMBS OF AN ADVENTURE)

Illustrations by Mark Millicent.

ISBN: 9781068517976

EGYPT
Scale 'n Miles
Littleton
and
Hackney's Route
1912
MEDITERRANEAN SEA
Sand
ARABIA PETRÆA
lots of Sand
lots more Sand
sand
Sand
CAIRO
Sand
Sand
lots more Sand
LOWER EGYPT
SIDE EGYPT
OLD EGYPT
lots of Sand
The Valley where Everyone is buried
more mountains
sand
Sand
RED SEA
UPPER EGYPT
DIRT
Sand

Chapter One
A Change in Fortunes

'Take the detached finger and discard the nail. If a finger is not available, a large toe will suffice. Break at the joints or knuckles and add to the iodine.

Crush hard with the pestle, mixing in the warm honey and fresh badger stools until you have the smooth consistency of molasses.'

'What to do with your mummies parts' is the title of the yellow paged book from which Littleton reads aloud. Another equally well-worn antiquarian-looking volume lies on the desk before him entitled 'Mrs. Beeton's best mummy powder recipes and their uses.'

The year is 1912. The Titanic is newly completed as the world's largest ocean liner. Scott of the Antarctic was recently lost and is now presumed dead. Germany and Europe will soon be gearing up for a Great War - one of the very best.

It was a colourful time of human discovery. 1911, the previous year, Hiram Bingham had led an expedition in Peru that came across 'The Lost City of the Incas' Machu Picchu. He had found another several years earlier called Hinky Bongo, but it didn't grab the public's imagination like Picchu. News of the discovery spread like wildfire at a time when the fastest method of communication was the telegraph and the early telephone.

Avidly read newspapers covered it far and wide, adding to the media frenzy, the publishing world was, at the time, the internet of yesteryear. If you wanted to know more about something, you would read a paper.

The world was changing: Queen Victoria relinquished her post as empress of India and has been dead for the last eleven years. Wilber Wright, who, along with his brother Orville, had built the very first aeroplane to sustain manned flight, had been buried a few short weeks ago on a bitterly cold morning in the spring, humankind unaware at that point how their invention would open the door for world travel to every far-flung corner of the globe. And aniseed gobstoppers are a shilling for a bag of twenty - chocolate mice, a halfpenny for two.

At the turn of the century, life was a cornucopia of ideals and extremes; it was a Giddy, Golden, Gilded, Golly Gosh Age!

Amidst these distractions, Egypt fever has the nation in its grip - the growing fascination with 'derring-do' and all things both old and new. Despite the bright spot of the Titanic's completion and successful sea trials, it is offset by Scott's disappointing bid for the South Pole.

Still, at present, science and discovery hold everyone spellbound. No man, woman, or small child can make it through the day without thinking of something innovatively new or, conversely, something old, mummified, petrified, or stuffed. The 20th century is barely in its teens. Like a child eager to discover the unknown world out there.

Curious people are always hungry for interesting 'stuff.' That childlike curiosity, inquisitiveness, and innovative grasp constantly reaching further, always looking beyond his imagination. It is an adventure that is the stuff of popular fare. This quest for knowledge at present knows no bounds. The nascent fruits of his labour are chronicled in many avidly read pamphlets and magazines of the day. One such publication and a good place to begin the start of our story is, 'A History Weekly.'

The popular publication is an everyday account of the newest archaeological finds, discoveries, and inventions. Foreign tropical expeditions and daring subcontinental Himalayan treks, the jungles, the deserts, and the oceans are all covered extensively. Exotic faraway places are brought to life and printed in vivid detail, sometimes with illustrations for the average Joe, found in most bookstores and barrows on any given Thursday, priced at just a shiny sixpence.

Archaeology: The future holds another decade of searching before Tutankhamun would be discovered in the Valley of the Kings by the Englishmen Lord Carnarvon and the illustrator Howard Carter. By the time that occurs, Charlie Chaplin will be the biggest global star on the planet, making more money than the Great War was costing to fund. In all facets of life, man was making ever greater headway and huge strides. Science, discovery and invention. Each step was greater than the last, and the public wanted to hear about it. Boy, did they ever!

The times, they were a changing.

Archaeology (the very word) evokes thoughts of men in funny hats digging for ancient things in faraway foreign places. But the era's romance is yet to translate from pure treasure hunting to a proper level of scientific study. This is the story of two men's participation in long-forgotten, little-known events that were to make that translation... imperative.

****

A typical steel grey day in the west end district of the city. At 17 Beak Street, London, several damp pigeons take shelter from the continuous drizzle on the window ledge of a drab soot-engrained five-story building. A dark but characterful building within which we find the rundown headquarters of Jameson and Co. Periodicals. Home to 'A History Weekly.' One of the many small publication houses that have sprung up in recent years. Horse hooves clad with shoes and metaled buggy wheels on the cobbles can be heard above the noise of the day's downpour. The hub of the glorious British Empire pulsating with the morning traffic.

On the third floor, in a rear office behind a frosted glass bearing their names, sit Larry Littleton and Harry Hackney, contributing sub-editor and assistant contributing sub-editor and illustrator. They are both engaged in their latest editorial articles. In keeping with the public's appetite of the moment, they write about Egypt. Though, to be honest, neither knows much about the specifics of the subject matter, as any cursory reading of their work would determine.

The two men toil together in the dimly lit wood- panelled room as they do daily. A grime-coated, single sash window provides light and looks out onto the building opposite. The flickering gaslight casts a yellow-toothed glow on the street below as the day begins to fade. The walls are a jumble of pinned articles and copy-proofs. A few childlike drawings of the pyramids that have, in fact, been executed by Hackney serve to showcase his limitations as an artist rather than any profound drafting skill.

Both men sit behind well-worn wooden desks. It is a room filled with unruly papers and old scattered books as jumbled as their thoughts. It is a place of subdued potential. A large white-faced wooden clock ticks loudly above a 
gilded framed picture of the king. Tidiness is not a habit in this office, as is productive work of any worth. Today, both men give the outward appearance of productivity. The leather-bound book from which Littleton reads aloud is worn and well-fingered, but its tired, yellowing pages have him enthralled, nonetheless. The book, like its surroundings, has seen better days.

'Can you believe it? People use these concoctions to cure illness, Hackney.' He looks across to his partner, Hackney, for some response. It is not forthcoming. In appearance, the two men could not be more dissimilar. Littleton, tall and thin with a pale, angular, almost boyish face, his manner is obstinate and needlessly meticulous. He is prone to high-pitched wails of agitation when provoked. He has another idiosyncrasy, a rather annoying nasal tick almost as regular as a mechanical timepiece. His overriding ambition is to be a real explorer like his mother and great aunty Eunice before him. For now, he is happy to console himself, delivering other people's adventures on the pages of 'A History Weekly.'

Hackney, by contrast, was a short barrel of a man. British bulldogs are built in the same mold. He has a certain style coupled with a chronic sweet tooth. He erroneously believes himself, without factual basis, to be quite a charmer with the ladies - this author can verify - he is not. Both men sport large, full-waxed moustaches, as is the fashion of the time. Generally, both work in rolled shirt sleeves anchored by elastic braces. Littleton wears a monogrammed leather visor above his spectacles.

It makes him feel like an editor: Today, he feels like an editor.

Hackney can say nothing as his current preoccupation continues to envelop him fully. His goal was to chase a ball-breaking aniseed-flavoured gobstopper around his mouth and between his teeth with his tongue. His self- set task was to force out every last atom of remaining flavour to be savoured and enjoyed.

He is absorbed.

Littleton puts down the book that has been holding his attention thus and switches it to Hackney. He watches, folding his arms and leaning back on his chair. Watching, and studying his partner as a fox might study a chicken dressed for dinner. Hackney's extreme facial contortions and exertions finally conspire to force the gobstopper violently from his mouth with a loud **POP!** He sends it bullet-like into his typewriter, where it firmly lodges itself between the keys and his current article.

Hackney looks up and registers his partner's disapproving sigh against him. He sets about the task of trying to extricate his trapped confectionery from within his typewriter with the aid of a pencil.

The office tannoy crackles into life, and a woman's voice of no discernible age requests that, 'Mr. Jameson would like to see

Larry Littleton and Harry Hackney in his office. Larry and Harry to Mr. Jameson's office now, please.'

Switching his attention from Harry, Littleton looks up at the speaker on the wall. 'Do you hear that, Harry? The chief, old Jameson himself, wants to see us in his office.'
'I smell promotion,' Hackney smiles.

Littleton sparkles with anticipation, removing his visor and placing both thumbs in his waistcoat pockets. He stands and gazes out of the window for a moment behind the desk. The bustling, animated street holds his attention. Horse-drawn buggies trundle by, some having to dance around the stuttering motorised vehicles as they cough and splutter, their drivers slowed by the blinkered trotting horses sharing the narrow streets and lanes. The turn-of-the-century roads are littered with piles of fresh horse dung that steam in the cold evening air all along the narrow thoroughfare. Good for the roses, but bad for the roads.

'The world is changing all too quickly, Hackney old chum,'
Larry says thoughtfully.
'I suppose at some point, all the history will have been discovered, and there will be no need for serious journalists like us, eh? Maybe, someday, there will be a magic portal to all the news and world events taking place; you will only need to push

a button or pull a switch to get it.' Harry retorts.
'Fanciful thinking, Hackney, my man, but there will always be a
need for journalists like us and as for your magic portal with all
the news at the push of a button or the flick of a switch, I'd say
it's the stuff of daydreams - there is more chance of a man
landing on the moon,' Larry declares.

Hackney smiles at the thought.

'You're right, of course. What do you suppose he wants?' asks
Hackney without looking up. He is still concentrating on
retrieving his trapped confectionery from his typewriter.
'Well, if you ask me, those last two articles we handed in for the
Thursday publication were pretty good; praise be where praise
is due,' waxes Littleton.

The rain begins to pour at a more torrential rate outside, and
several pigeons stare contemptuously back at him from the
window ledge.

'I have to agree with you, Littleton, although it's a shame we
never made the Wednesday deadline for publication. You don't
suppose he's still annoyed at that, do you?'

'No. I think, on the whole, he recognises talent when he sees it.
It's just unfortunate that we do seem to miss so many print
deadlines,' Littleton sniffs, 'I think this place owes some of its
success to our contributions to this publication, our intuitive

know-how and journalistic flair, and your wonderfully descriptive illustrations,' he adds.

'Yes, as usual, you are probably right again,' Hackney sighs and nods in agreement. His countenance is almost the mirror opposite of his partner. A confident yet confused demeanour in an impractical but willing sort of way.

The two men work equally, but both are devoid of efficiency as an unlikely team. Both graduated from Life's University of Ineptitude with first-class honours and are now gainfully employed at the London office of 'A History Weekly,' however, contrary to those positions, their lack of the relevant qualifications might seem to the casual observer.

Both men, now brimming with confident anticipation, 'To the chief!' the two men shout, heading out the door and upstairs to the office of Wallace W. Jameson, proprietor and editor-in-chief of Jameson Periodicals.

Jameson's office is a stark contrast to Littleton and Hackney's workplace. Everything in it is neat, set in an orderly manner, with volumes of books all shelved alphabetically and by size. Wooden filing cabinets hide any unruly paperwork. It is a very much larger affair. Three large sash windows serve to illuminate the more opulent surroundings.

The noise from the street five floors below is barely audible above the ticking of the clock. The clock that has beneath it a portrait of Jameson himself, if a rather more flattering rendition. Staring down from a small, gilded frame at Littleton and Hackney, they stand in front of a very expansive leather top desk.

Both men stare silently at the back of a winged button-swivel chair. The man who puffs heavily with clenched teeth on a cheap Havana behind that desk and sat in that chair was Wallace. W. Jameson. A robust northern businessman who had founded the small print shop on a frugal footing many years earlier. The soul components were no-nonsense, no nose hair, and the much-fingered lid to a 'Malty's fish paste jar' that had served to remind him of his working-class roots.

The canny investment strategy of Wallace. W. Jameson had grown the thriving publication business into what it is today. He had hoped that one day a son and heir would inherit the family business - but alas, he had fathered only daughters with his long-suffering wife Bernice. A comely woman but thunderously dull and devoid of much that is commonly called intelligence. Many of the firm's employees took great pleasure in her visits to the premises as it was not uncommon to be able to trick her into removing her undergarments under the pretence that it was company policy.

Having married Jameson many years her senior, it was not an unpleasant enterprise, and it was even rumoured that some had taken the game one step further. Today, Wallace W. Jameson puffed angrily on his cheap cigar and checked the status of his bright ginger hairpiece upon his very shiny head. After a long minute, the rosy red-faced jowls of Jameson spins slowly around to address the two standing employees, cigar smoke billows hanging heavily in the air. Penetrative eye contact is made, but no words are spoken. Littleton and Hackney exchange glances as Jameson begins his address.

'Ah, Gentlemen, why do you suppose I wish to see you two today?' The fact that these words are uttered through firmly clenched teeth alters Littleton's first summation that this would be a positive meeting. By way of tactics, Littleton decides to make an upfront apology.

'If it's about your wife's visit last week, sir, it was all something of a misunderstanding, so I can only say that I am not fully to blame, but how sorry we both are. Very sorry for the incident that occurred. We will, of course, pay for the staining and any further cleaning costs that may have been incurred.' Jameson's frown deepens.

'My wife? My wife? You blithering idiot, this has nothing to do with my wife,' his long sigh is not missed. 'Let's try another one. Why do you suppose you are employed here?'

Jameson's eyes harden to a glare. Tired and fatigued by an endless battle he knows he can never win; he continues to answer his own question. 'It is because, Mr. Littleton, you are Lady Winterbottom's nephew, a wonderful woman, and shareholder in this company,' he rises from the desk and draws himself up to his full 5'4", striding around the desk and placing himself between the two humbled employees. So close they could distinctly smell the soured herring salad on his breath that he had consumed for lunch at the Firkin Gherkin restaurant next door.

'Lady Winterbottom and I have an understanding and unfortunately ... well, you unfortunately are a part of that understanding,' he grimaces. 'Understand?'

Littleton winces at the well-aimed barrage of putdowns.

'And you, Mr. Hackney, as fate would have it, are my nephew.' A forced smile is drawn again across his lips. 'Your dear departed father would not want you destitute,' he sighs again, then, without warning, explodes, startling Littleton and Hackney to the point of a particularly nasty bout of involuntary flatulence. 'Which is what you will both be unless you come up with something that is remotely readable and contains at least one believable fact or bone of interest to our readers,' he seethes.

His animated outburst had caused his opulent mane of artificial hair to wander from its original position and it now lingered, comically, a fraction above his right eye. He frowned, waiting for either man to dare mention it. W. Jameson was a man who called a spade a spade and took no nonsense. Except, that is, where Littleton and Hackney were concerned. His dalliance with Lady Winterbottom and the promise he had made to his dear departed brother were beginning to strangle him with a throttling grip.

Today, he will release that grip and will put an end to the nonsense he has suffered at the hands of the two most inept employees he has ever had the misfortune to hire.

Taking stock, speaking in measured tones, he addresses Littleton first, 'Mr. Littleton, if I said your last submitted article lacked the rudiments of any factual credibility, what would you think?'

'You mean in a good way?' Silence.
'Have you read it, sir?' asks Littleton, rather unsure.

'Not in its entirety, but let's go over it together, shall we?' he smiles.

Littleton mistakes Jameson's patronising manner for genuine interest and smiles back in agreement. From the pocket of his jacket, Jameson produces a piece of paper that shows severe signs of wear and tear, almost as if it had been screwed up into a tiny ball. Pushing the bridge of his spectacles closer with one finger and flicking the hair that has now made its way down to just above his right eye, he begins to read aloud from it.

'Companions of Rameses the second's brother Desmond.' Looking up from the paper, he repeats the two syllables slowly. 'Des-mond, an unusual name for a pharaoh, Desmond?' handing the paper back to Littleton to continue reading. He sits back at his desk. Enthusiastically, Littleton takes off.

'Well, chief, I have translated some newly discovered hieroglyphics in conjunction with some old, nearly ancient hieroglyphics, coupled with my findings using some intuitive guesswork based on some coincidentally previously overlooked facts that have recently come to light. I have come up with the not-too-far-fetched notion that may lead us to the spiritual and personal companions of Rameses, the second's little heard-of brother, Desmond.'

'This is fantastic,' comments Jameson with an air of sarcasm that is completely lost on Littleton. Jameson's response only serves to bolster his enthusiasm as he smiles back and continues, 'Mousy Mouse and Goldy Fish swimmer of the

Nile?' Jameson takes a deep breath. 'I see. Were these people of royal patronage? His servants? Maybe his Temple friends?'

'No, sir, not people at all, that's why these facts are being overlooked, they were in actuality   ' he pauses for effect. 'His pets, his royal pets.' With a satisfied beam on his face, Littleton awaits the chief's reply.

'So let me see if I understand you correctly, 'Mousy Mouse' was a mouse. A royal rodent? And 'Goldy Fish' swimmer of the Nile would be his goldfish?'
'My translations lead me to believe this to be the case,' Littleton replies, smiling confidently.
'You idiot,' is Jameson's reply.

The clock ticks loudly as if the exchange hadn't occurred. Jameson turns to Hackney, whose concentration is channelled toward the release of flavour from a freshly installed gobstopper.

'Hackney, you're a clever fellow, perhaps you can explain this article of yours about the Wasabi desert mummies already discovered. I'm probably misunderstanding it somewhere, but from what I can make of it, your theory states that they were just severe sunburn cases?' Reading from a different piece of similarly damaged paper, he struggles with Hackney's typing, which is on a skill level roughly equivalent to his artwork.

'As I read on, you state that some of these unfortunates may have been staggering around lost in the desert with such severe sunburn that they fell into some badger holes in the ground and died and then dried. Died then dried... turning into mummies with brown hard skin?'

Hackney starts to say something, but thinks better of it and remains silent as he notices Jameson's left eye beginning to twitch ominously, which is always a bad sign.

'Would you say there were many of your burrowing badgers in the desert at around the time of the second dynasty, Hackney?' Hackney stares back blankly. 'Listen, you two! Do you honestly think you deserve another chance to write something that this newspaper can print?'

Both men beam back at him expectantly in the affirmative.

These words are remarkably audible for a man speaking through clenched teeth. He glances at Hackney, who has begun to fold the piece of paper that was stuck firmly between the keys of his typewriter moments before.

'I'd like to see what you're working on at the moment,' he gestures for the messy piece of paper.
'Oh, it's nothing, sir,' Hackney murmurs, slipping the paper quickly into his pocket.

'I know it will be nothing, but I'd like to see it all the same.'

Holding out his hand. Hackney sheepishly complies. The paper is torn and dirty in the centre, which looks like a reddish-brown stickiness as Jameson gingerly touches it. And raises his finger to his nose. 'Aniseed, sir.' Hackney quickly interrupts Jameson's examination of his work. 'Aniseed, of course.'

All three men stare into space, in silence. The only sound was the loud ticking of the clock and the grinding of Jameson's teeth. The awkward moment is thankfully broken by the tannoy again fluttering into life.

'There is a Miss Elizabeth Fern to see Mr. Jameson.' Jameson looks up from the desk.
The voice from the speaker then adds as an after- thought, 'She is quite posh.' Jameson looks back at the two men. He glares at the piece of paper in his hand before handing it back to Hackney.

'Two words, gentlemen. You two are fired! I said it; what a relief. You're fired, both of you, you're fired, get out! Oh, that sounds good now. Get out, clear your desks, pack your things, and be gone! Good day, gentlemen, and good riddance!' He drops back down into his comfortable leather chair while his hairpiece sits comically out of place, almost giggling with relief.

Littleton and Hackney are dumb-struck, hit by a thunderbolt at Jameson's words; they stare at the back of the chair. Cigar smoke billows furiously from behind it. Littleton's eyes begin to well with tears; never did either man expect to lose his job for something as trivial as not being able to do it. Littleton contemplates attempting to protest, but it is useless.

'Out, out, out! You are fired, Gentlemen.'

They turn dejectedly to slowly shuffle out of the office, crestfallen, shocked, and unemployed.

Back in the tiny room that had been their former workplace and home, Littleton and Hackney start to remove the trappings that had added a personal flavour to their otherwise dim surroundings. Hackney's renderings of the great pyramids, some boiled sweets, his dried wasp collection, a lucky pumice stone, and an ugly-shaped dry potato that made him giggle every time he looked at it, except today.

He did not smile at the potato today. It just made him feel sad.

Littleton's retrievals were equally pathetic. A stuffed woodcock
in a small, cracked case, some strangely titled books inside,
which he had concealed some unusual photographs of semi-
naked ladies between several of the folded back pages. An old
spring mouse trap that, over many years, had given him great
amusement as he had tried to outwit it.

The two men stood together at the window. The drawers were
all cleared, and the contents were in boxes. One last look at the
view.

'Dash it all,' sighs Hackney.
'If only we could've come up with something to impress
Jameson. Something he would've been proud of.' Littleton
shakes his head.
'Yes, but you can't do a lot in such a short period; three years is
not enough for anyone to make their mark.'
'Too true, Hackney old friend. What were you working on?
What was on that paper?'
'I was working on 'R',' replied Hackney. 'Ah RA, the sun god,
it's pronounced Ra.' 'No,' Hackney retorts.
'Yes, the Sun god, Ra of Egypt and all that.'

'No, I was working on the letter R, it sticks on my typewriter. Loosening it up.'

He hands over the piece of paper to Littleton who eyes the article in question. The only letter on the page on the crumpled piece of paper was an 'R' for half a page, punctuated with a brown-reddish smear of gobstopper dribble.

'I see, not one of your most successful articles, is it?' he said dryly, glancing at the clock, it was almost 6 o'clock. The air of despondency was broken by the pinstripe reemergence of Wallace W. Jameson. He seemed less rageful, almost pleasant, standing at the office door with what could just pass for a smile on his face.

'Before you make any hasty decisions. I've come to apologise,' the words out of his mouth don't come easily. He holds in his hands a folded telegram. 'I may have spoken a little hastily.' Hackney and Littleton exchange optimistic glances.
'An opportunity has arisen for 'A History Weekly' to cover the Lord Fern's sponsorship dinner, and there's no one else available at such short notice, so reluctantly, I'm assigning you two.'
'Then we're not fired?' Hackney asks. 'Who said anything about you being fired?' 'You did,' both men answer.

Jameson pauses, barely controlling a strange, suppressed, almost maniacal giggle that does its best to slip from his lips as if he has no control over them. He straightens his tie, fixes his concentration on the two men with a more than usual glare and then continues.

'Tonight, Lord Fern will announce who will receive his coveted award of sponsorship towards the expedition to Egypt in search of the lost Chantress of Asanti. The discovery of which will be a crowning achievement in a long and distinguished career in Egyptology, not to mention the savoury cracker business.' As a strained but resigned afterthought, he adds, 'I know I can rely on you two.' Again, the suppressed cackle is almost painfully controlled.

'I know I can rely on you two to cover the story accurately and concisely.' These last two details are spoken slowly and with great measure. Jameson stares squarely at a nervous Littleton and a bowed Hackney. The large mahogany clock with its beating tick punctuated their breathing.

Wallace W. Jameson pulls from his pinstripe waistcoat pocket a gold fob watch, flicks it open, and checks the time with the clock on the wall.

'The dinner is at eight, don't be late. Hampstead Gardens. Violet has the details.' He moves to exit the room, then, as an afterthought, turns to the two men. 'Do not, and I repeat, do not bollocks this up.'

'You'll get no bollocks from us, sir. You can rely on us, that you can.'

Jameson turns his back on them and leaves the room, it was difficult to tell if he was laughing or crying as he wandered off.

Chapter Two
The Dinner

Lord Fern was in possession of a vital clue that could shed light on the last resting place of the first handmaiden of Princess Pal-Perie the Third. Otherwise known as the Chantress of Asante.

The Temple of Asante was originally the top-notch Temple for chanting on the banks of the mother Nile at the time. About 1500 BC, chanting was a lucrative business. In those days, every ceremony needed some good chanting. A ceremony was nothing without the services of a talented chantress. Weddings, funerals, ritual sacrifices, chantresses made more than chanters and were more pleasing to the eye. To be chief Chantress of Asante was a big kudos and a very important role in the funerary arrangement business of the period.

One of the many perks that came with the job, along with summer hours and meal coupons, was an ample supply of the exalted ceremonial funeral biscuits known as 'chanting crackers.'

Its origins can be found in the little-known sister book to 'The Book of the Dead' - Its sister book being, 'The Book of the Bread,' or as it became more commonly known, the 'Chronicle of the Cracker.' An ancient Egyptian collection of mortuary texts and magic formulas placed in tombs and believed to protect and preserve the deceased in the hereafter with the use of light savoury snacks.

These crackers were light, dry biscuit snacks that were shared and broken in a symbolic act of feasting. Simple dry bread effects that could be made more palatable with the addition of butter and Nile jam. Shared around the temple after the proceedings, the crackers had helped her gain a fair measure of popularity amongst the temple-goers.

Temple Dancers

Legend has it that the chief cracker maker passed on his
methods and ingredients only to the Chantress, and with each
new Chantress came a new cracker. But it was the crackers of
Asante that would become legendary. Nobody knows quite
why it was that the crackers of Asanti were so exalted; maybe it
was because they were just that little extra salted? Some say they
were possibly more salty, some say the packaging may have
been more colourful, some say maybe they were less salty, and
some say it looks like rain when it really doesn't.

But whatever the reason, it is now lost to the sands of time. The
secrets of that rarest of cracker biscuits went to her grave and
were buried along with her as was the custom and part of the
funerary ritual of the Ancient Kingdoms at the time.

Over the intervening centuries and rolling millennia, The
Chantress and her exact last resting place were lost to sands of
antiquity. Many had searched for the fabled crackers of Asanti.
None had ever been successful.

****

Dusk has turned to darkness, and both men, now dressed for dinner, are sat in the back of a horse-drawn Hansom cab. The clip of horse hooves echoed clear on the night air. Littleton looked the more dapper of the two, sporting a smart cape, and cane as is the current fashion. While Hackney is attired in more conventional woollen tweed and an overcoat. Neither pays much attention to the journey as the grand houses of Bishops Avenue pass by on either side. Each house is more extravagant than the last.

'Remember what Jameson said clearly, accurately, and concisely. Have you remembered your notebook?' Littleton asks of Hackney.
'Damn. Have you?' Hackney replies. Both men realise they have forgotten their tools of the trade.
'You are supposed to be my illustrator; how can you sketch things down if you don't bring your pad?' 'Ah, Fiddlesticks... but I do work from memory.' 'You work from memory in a book you have forgotten?'

As if to justify his possession of it, Littleton uses his cane to tap the wooden partition between themselves and the cab driver.

'I say, driver, I say driver, you wouldn't have a notebook and pencil with you that we could borrow?'

Hackney chews on his last piece of fudge after offering it to
Littleton. 'Fraid not, governor, not a lot of call for notebooks.'

The driver mumbles something indiscernible under his breath,
but the phrase 'kin' stupid toffs' can be heard quite clearly...

Littleton eyes the crumpled brown paper bag that contains
Hackney's fudge pieces.
'If worst comes to worst, we will use it for notes.' 'Good idea,'
Hackney responds.
He pushed the last few pieces of fudge in his mouth, thus freeing
the bag to take any pertinent notes on.
'Do you suppose they will have some crisps and biscuits?'
'I don't know, Hackney, I haven't been to many award dinners.
You would think so, wouldn't you?'
' ... maybe some of those little warm pastries too?' Littleton
continues.

Even though it is now dark as they approach Fern Manor, it is
clear that it is a substantial estate. The caped and hatted
gateman holding a lantern waves them through, and they pass
him without stopping. The loose gravel crunches beneath the
spoked wooden wheels of the carriage as they travel the dark
driveway. Flanked by lawns and cedar trees, fountains, and
statues, opulence, and money permeate the cold night air.

As they draw closer to the house, it is an austere and very grand affair that greets them. A gothic stately home with a large three-tiered marbled stone fountain - the centre piece of a circular driveway. Some of the other guests' transport and drivers have parked up and are waiting. The working men, the drivers, chat amongst themselves.

The two reporters disembark the carriage and ascend several stone steps leading up to a set of large, solid panel doors, more in keeping with the entrance to a church than someone's place of residence. The black cast-iron doorbell is fashioned in the form of a sphinx. It is operated by pulling its hinged head forward. This greatly amuses Hackney, who is much taken with its novelty and realism.

'Good golly, a sphinx doorbell. Well, well, well, I say, whatever next, Littleton?'

The two men stand in the chill evening mist, stamping their feet and blowing into their cupped hands as they await an answer. After a moment, the door is answered by a young woman in a crisp starched maid's uniform and mob hat.
'Good evening, madam.'

That is all Littleton manages to say as a large brown feathery object hurtles out of the night, straight into the back of his head. The force of the impact is such that it knocks him completely off his feet. To render him quite unconscious and sprawled at the feet of both the open-mouthed maid and the only slightly less startled Hackney. His hat knocked several feet inside the parquet-floored hallway. The maid and Hackney are left staring down at Littleton's prostrate body. Hackney, being only slightly startled, regains his composure almost without missing a beat. He removes his hat and picks up where Littleton left off.

'Good evening, Miss, how do you do? I'm afraid my companion has been knocked silly by... ' he bends down and picks up the seemingly lifeless body of a rather moth-eaten scruffy tawny owl. The old owl still has a mouse clamped firmly between its talons and both now show all the outward signs of life having left them.

'This owl... we do have an appointment.' The maid closes her mouth, taking Hackney's offered business card, and opens the door more fully. The two of them struggle with the unconscious Littleton, finally seating him in a large, upholstered leather chair.

Hackney, as an afterthought, picks up the owl and places it in Littleton's lap. He then hands his hat and coat to the maid, who retreats with them down the corridor, bidding him follow. Still

a little flustered from the incident she has just witnessed, she looks back over her shoulder at the sleeping gentleman now cradling an owl.

'Will he be alright, sir?'

'Oh, I should think so, tough as old boots some of these birds.'

'The rest is through 'ere sir,' the maid speaks with a strong South London accent, to which Hackney smiles politely.

Through 'ere is an immense drawing-room, opulently furnished and bathed in the warm glow from a crackling fire nestled in a fire-dogged hearth beneath a large marble surround. The vaulted room is filled with people whom Hackney presumes are prominent archaeologists.

Lord Fern is seated and easily identifiable in a wicker bath chair. His appearance is something of a shock, a frail white-haired old man holding in his hand a large ear trumpet that he points in every direction, trying to latch on to any conversation. The Lord is surrounded by several doctors and professors, all looking eagerly to be bestowed the gift of sponsorship. The chatter goes silent as Hackney makes his way across the room.

All talking stops. He is eyed warily. Besides himself, he counts nine other men, one of whom sits alone in front of the fire.

'How do you do, Lord Fern,' Hackney holds out his hand to the geriatric gentleman. 'The name's Hackney, I'm here as a reporter,' continuing to hold out his hand confidently.

'You don't look anything like her,' retorts the Lord, straining hard, looking more than slightly puzzled. 'My daughter, why are you here as her if you are a man? Tell me that?'

Hackney stares around the room and can tell from everyone's reaction that they are also aware that the Lord was playing with less than a full deck. The moment is broken by a loud, shrill shriek that comes from beyond the room.

It comes from somewhere down the hallway. Intense and girl-like, it was, of course, Littleton having come to and regained consciousness at about the same time as the owl. Both are now equally shocked at each other's close company. The owl so much so that it released its grip on the mouse, which was not so dead as the initial inspection may have led Hackney to believe.

Now, all three are moving at speed in various directions from where Hackney had left them. Heavy footsteps rapidly approach the open doors to the drawing room. Littleton appears and checks himself; his body gives the appearance of being stationary, but the momentum he has gained in his hurry to escape the company of the owl and the mouse propels him in the most graceful glide across the polished floor at what appears to be around 30 miles an hour.

His open-eyed gaze is met by the collective amazement of the assembled men of science. The owl maintains its speed and in its panic flies over Littleton's head straight into the face of a beautiful ornate carved grandfather clock, causing it to sway ever so slightly and topple, then crash forward onto the floor.

It was that bloody large owl!

The springs and chimes of the ancient timepiece, echoing its last death, rattle around the room. Coupled with the odd crackle from the fire, the silence was the only sound to be heard in the moments after the clock's demise. Everyone stands and stares first at the remains of the clock, then finally resting their gaze on an open-mouthed Littleton. With a slight nasal tick and a light brushing down, Littleton nervously runs his fingers through his hair and approaches the group just a little self-consciously.

'Good evening, my Lord; sorry about your owl.' The wings of which protruded from beneath the clock spreadeagled.
'I mean your clock. I'm Laurence Littleton from 'A History Weekly'. I'm here as a reporter.'

The Lord raises his ear trumpet, wide-eyed and frowns. 'I've only got one and neither of you two imposters looks anything

like her at all.' He thunders back as much as he is able to
thunder.

This reply takes Littleton as much by surprise as it did
Hackney. He looks around the room for a clue. The group casts
exasperated eyes at the ceiling almost in unison. This initial
exchange leads Littleton to conclude that the Lord no longer
has both oars in the water as the fire crackles, the clock no
longer ticks, and the evening continues.

'Can we please get on with the announcement?' The voice is
from no one in the group but emanates from behind a large
leather Chesterfield.

The lone figure.

Heads swivel and everyone turns to see who has spoken. A
gaunt, pale face with angular, stark features turns to stare back
at them with its piercing black eyes. The skull of a face forces a
cracked smile. The fire is a flickering glow.

The character has an intense quality in his stare that unnerves
each of those it rests on. Slowly, he raises himself from the
chair. Long spider legs reveal a very tall man, immaculately

dressed in a jacket and frock coat. It was hard to say how old he would be; he was not young, but neither was he old. Weathered and hard like a brittle stone garden statue, his chill, cold presence is felt all around the room. This man is Singleton Sinclair ...

'You would like that, wouldn't you?' This time, it is a woman's voice, deep and mysterious. Everyone's heads swivel again in unison, this time to see who had spoken, surprised by the femininity of it. Elizabeth Fern, the Lord's daughter, stands half in the room and half out of the room, smoking from a long cigarette holder. A spring in the clock goes off, and everyone checks their gaze back to Elizabeth as they all stare. Monocles are raised, and murmurs are murmured. Littleton and Hackney exchange a glance. They do not indeed bear any resemblance to the Lord's daughter.

She's a large woman, not unattractive, with lustrous ebony hair, bright scarlet painted lips, and a confidence born of aristocratic breeding. She has a strident countenance and amply filled her satin skirts that hid her legs from view. She sounds quite posh. Littleton can't help but feel he has met her before but dismisses the feeling fleetingly as just a quirk of imagined coincidence, Deja Vu.

The fire's comforting crackle is again interrupted by the same girl-like piercing scream that was heard earlier. People look at Littleton as the originator of the original, almost identical sound, but this scream was way off down the hall. Footsteps are again heard approaching rapidly. This time, it is the maid who passes into view and then flies past the open doors. Elizabeth stands at the entrance to the drawing room and watches the flashing black and white skirt and fluttering apron of the maid, screaming wildly as she passes.

'A mouse, a mouse!' the maid yells. Elizabeth turns and re-focuses, quick as a flash, bringing one of her not-in-substantial little feet crashing down on the pursuing small rodent with a sickening bone-grinding crunch.

Turning back to the flabbergasted group as if she did that every day, she smiles sweetly at the shocked attendees, revealing a fine and perfect set of pearl-white teeth. With a long draw on her cigarette, she addresses the group of scholarly gentlemen.

'Gentlemen... good evening.'

Elizabeth makes her way across the room; she is a big girl, but moved with the grace of a well-trained aristocratic feline. Collectively all eyes follow. Everyone is transfixed.

'Relax, gentlemen, I'm not going to eat you, Professor Joseph,' she smiles at one of the bespectacled attendees. 'Or you, Mr. Rankin.'

Looking at a rather nervous fellow mopping his head with his handkerchief. 'You all know me, I'm speaking for my father when I say we both thank all of you for coming along tonight,' she avoids looking towards the tall skull-featured man. He shows disinterest and stares further into the fire's coals.

'We may have sandwiches ... later,' she smiles to a murmur of approval.

'My father, your potential benefactor, has invited you all here tonight to announce the recipient of his generous sponsorship. One of you will be lucky enough to have more than ample funds to mount an expedition to Egypt to discover the High Chantress of Asante. The resultant exposure will make one of you a very important and most probably a famous person in your own right, no doubt. We can all agree that every man here hopes it will be him, as you are all equally qualified, and we must somehow select a winner. We have taken unusual steps to add an element of chance to the proceedings this evening. We have come up with the idea of a lottery.'

'A lottery!' came back the collectively shocked replies that were manifest in their incredulous tone. 'A lottery! In heaven's name have you taken leave of your senses?' called one dissenting voice from the group.

The attendant group is agitated, to say the least.

'What pottery?' the lone voice of the geriatric Lord Fern is heard to stutter as he shifts his ear trumpet around the room. 'Shut up, Daddy, I said lottery,' is her only curt reply. 'Each of you will be given a folded piece of paper, but only one of the pieces will have a mark. He who draws the paper with a mark is the winner.' She passes amongst them with a hat, handing out small pieces of folded paper until everyone in the room has one, including both Littleton and Hackney.

'Surely there is some mistake you have given the papers to the reporters too?'
'Yes, I don't see that there's any harm in it, do you? It's hardly likely they will win; I shouldn't worry about it,' she says firmly. 'And there's an end to it. All right, gentlemen, you may unfold your papers.'

Elizabeth turns her back on the group and pulls hard on a freshly lit cigarette as she stares into the crackling fire awaiting the inevitable uproar that she knows will come.

The man who had voiced his impatience and the lack of an announcement stands addressing Elizabeth, making himself heard.

'Wait a moment, this mark that tells us we have won, what is it?' It's Singleton Sinclair's voice that stares unemotionally at his folded piece of paper, his cold eyes glaring at the coals of the fire.

'A crushed scarab,' she utters the words without turning to face him. His reaction is instant; her words are like Hemlock to him. His eyes blaze. All heads in the room turn to Singleton Sinclair. Elizabeth, too, turns, finally looking in Sinclair's direction.
 'Do you know why I use that signature, The Scarab Beetle?' The attendees shake their heads and murmur.

'I will tell you,' Sinclair begins. 'It's because the ancient Egyptians revered the proud scarab as a potent symbol of rebirth and renewal. Laying his eggs to hatch inside the rolled balls of stinking, dung. Dung that he collected as he went on his way rolling it into perfect tiny spheres... round and round he would go using his hairy little beetle legs... I too have hairy legs,' he raises a trouser leg a few inches and reveals as much. The attendees look at the offered glimpse of Sinclair's revealed hairy ankle, feeling it would be rude not to.

'That gentleman - that is why I use the symbol as my signature.'

Each man, no wiser after Sinclair's explanation, nods in approval. He tears his paper slowly in half without looking at it, then addresses Elizabeth between heavy breaths, speaking slowly, getting louder as each word leaves his lips. 'You would mock me cleverly, or so you think.'
'I don't mean to, Sinclair, but if you should take offence, then so be it.'
'Elizabeth, everyone here knows my mark is the Scarab, a black scarab. It's my signature; people respect it, they respect me. Dealers, shippers, archivists, curators and auctioneers, circus performers, beekeepers and unicyclists.' He begins to boil furiously, 'So you would take me and crush me, would you? I don't think so.'

Hackney whispers quietly to Littleton, 'Did he say pea-keepers?'
'Beekeepers, he said beekeepers,' Littleton replies, somewhat irritated.

Sinclair's controlled rage is desperately trying to escape, but he has had years of practice keeping a restraint on it. He gives a slow, bony smile before throwing the torn pieces of paper onto the fire.

'I don't think so.' Singleton strides across the room, stepping over the clock. None of the other men try to stop him. 'Don't you want to know who has won?' asks Professor Joseph, a popular work colleague of the assembled group. He has a thick head of red hair and a strong Scottish accent as he takes Singleton's arm. Singleton turns and addresses the man standing in his way. The man quickly releases his hold on Singleton's sleeve.

'You fool, I know who has won,' with that, like a witch on her broom, he's gone from the room.

'There's always one that doesn't want to play. Mr. Sinclair. Hmm, I had no idea that he would assume a connection between such an obvious choice of imagery and his mark. That's why I steered clear from a simple duplication of the commonly used lower Nile symbol.' People don't look too convinced by her explanation. 'I didn't want to offend anyone.' She smiles sweetly.

Everyone looks to Elizabeth. Littleton and Hackney just look confused. The fire crackles. The clock ticks and the proceedings continue.

'Gentleman, open your papers, please.' Seconds later, a broad grin creeps over Littleton's face, his eyes widening as he looks over to see if Hackney is holding the piece of paper.

They both hold papers that bear the mark that Elizabeth had described. Hackney opens his and finds that he, too, has a crushed scarab symbol; as he scans the room, it becomes apparent that everyone else has drawn blanks. Quickly, he screws up and thrusts the piece of paper into his pocket and ushers Hackney to do the same, but it is too late as Hackney is already announcing his good fortune.

'I say, sorry to spoil the proceedings, but unfortunately, I seem to have drawn the beetle, so to speak.' Sheepishly, Hackney holds up the paper with the mark for all to see.
 'Then you have won,' she responds calmly, awaiting the inevitable uproar. She does not wait long.
'Why, this is outrageous; what do you think you were doing?' Dr Rankin asks.

Woken by the noise, the sleeping Lord looks around the room at the shouting group of men. Lord Fern is now invigorated by the noise and rest from his light sleep. He notices, then stares hard at the defunct timepiece on the floor.

'What's that chicken doing under my clock there is nothing for him there,' he warbles as he glares at the owl that still remains spreadeagled beneath the silent timepiece. The Lord has not been keeping track of the evening's proceedings.

'My Lord, Lady Elizabeth has given your sponsorship to one of the reporters. Are you not going to do something to stop your daughter's madness?'

The geriatric Lord's only reaction is to raise one of his white bushy eyebrows, making one of his eyes appear inordinately larger than the other. He then leans heavily on his left elbow, smiles and releases an exceedingly loud bout of flatulence with a beaming grin of relief. Very proud of himself, he sinks back into his chair with the words 'Better out than in... '.

'Then so be it, I will not be made a fool of. Good night, gentlemen,' Dr Rankin strides from the room as did Singleton before him, stepping over the clock. Followed one by one as the others leave, each voicing their anger and disappointment in various tones of discontent. Unmoved as they pass a sincerely unemotional Elizabeth Fern, who bids them goodnight.

'You have wasted all our time; we won't forget this.'
'It's disgraceful,' someone adds as he makes his way across the room.

A gentleman who is the last to leave turns to give his voice, repeating only what others have said, but adds, 'and we didn't get any sandwiches,' then, just like the rest, is gone.

The room is again quiet.

There is an air of subdued confusion, and a slight smell of cabbage lingers.

Elizabeth's features transform when she turns her attention to the two reporters, smiling at Littleton and Hackney. They are the only ones left, not knowing quite how to react, they smile back. Lord Fern has gone to sleep and dozes peacefully. Littleton clears his throat and glances in Hackney's direction. 'Clearly, accurately, and concisely bollocks-ed that up, didn't we?'
'Indeed, I would say so, I would indeed,' replies Hackney.

Chapter Three
The Assignment

'The fools they think
I don't know,' smiles
Elizabeth Fern with
satisfaction.
She stands in front of
the glowing fire;
behind her, the
embers in the hearth warm her ample behind. A striking,
formidable, and clever woman by any standards. She watches
Hackney and Littleton as the two hapless reporters remain
silent. The two men linger beside a large bookcase, unsure of
what to do.

'Come over here, don't be shy, well done,' she smiles as she
thrusts forward her equally ample bosom... and she sounds very
posh.

It is Littleton who speaks first.

'Miss Fern, why did we win? It wasn't fair that both of us had
the mark on our papers.' Hackney looks surprised at this news.
'We're reporters, journalists.' Littleton is somewhat intimidated
by her gaze and can't shake the distinct feeling that he has met
her before.

'There is no mistake, certainly not on your part. I knew of Singleton's contrived plan to pay off whoever received the grant money for the expedition sponsorship, and they, in turn, would make the discovery using my father's funds. While my father would fail to gain the recognition that would rightfully be his. The plan he had laid out is something I cannot and will not let happen. I need someone who will stay loyal to my father and discover the Lost Chantress of Asante in his name for him.' 'Do you take us for fools, Miss Fern?' Hackney asks.

'Yes,' she replies, smiling confidently. Her attention is more focused on the hearth of the fire.

'I see,' says Hackney, looking a little perplexed, then downright confused as to what their next move should be.

'With your help, it would be a fitting crown to my father's career,' she smiles at the frail old man asleep comfortably in his chair by the fire. 'Molly, the maidservant whom you met earlier tonight, learned of this dastardly plan from a confidence in service at another household. Those who were here tonight were to go against my father. The name of the dinner host who laid this plan was... ' she pauses, looking around the room for some unseen interloper before continuing.

'Singleton Sinclair. It was he who held a dinner party last Thursday. His plot was relayed to me and his dastardly and fiendish intentions laid bare.'

'Do tell,' whispers Littleton as he is quite taken with their captivating host and her intriguing tale.

****

THE PREVIOUS THURSDAY

It is the evening of the previous Thursday. Outside a substantial five-floored porticoed house in the vicinity of Regent's Park, a carriage comes to a stop. The home is an immaculate example of Georgian architecture at its finest. Bathed in the yellow glow of the lighted street lamps, the London Plane tree's leafless branches cast flickering spider-web shadows across its pale stucco walls.

Professor Joseph and Mr. Rankin step from the footplate of a drawn carriage. Joseph pays the driver a clean shilling and the men check out the home, both impressed by its grandeur.

'It will be interesting to hear what Sinclair has to say; he's summoned us here so mysteriously. Your invitation bore his mark as did mine.' Professor Joseph says, holding it up to the light from the gas lantern, both contemplate the insignia of

a black scarab beetle embossed on the paper. Joseph returns it
to his overcoat pocket before turning to Rankin.

'Have you heard who else will be attending tonight?' Rankin is
dressed for the cold, wears a large grey overcoat, and a
matching Homburg. He smiles as Professor Josephs raises his
collar against the chill evening air.
'I have not, but it's a rare thing when Singleton sends out dinner
invitations. I only knew you were attending by our chance
meeting at the museum.'
'I do hope he has some crisps and biscuits and things,' adds
Rankin.
Joseph nods, 'Some cake and sandwiches would be nice.' 'Yes, I
like cake too.'

The maid answers the door. With a friendly smile, she enquires
of the two gentlemen their names. They all take the chance to
chat about how cold the weather is for this time of year while
taking the two men's hats and bidding them entry into a warmer
sanctuary.

The house itself is a museum. Egyptian artefacts as far as the
eye can see. If you didn't know, you could have sworn you were
in the Egyptian section of the British Museum. Standing
sarcophagi and golden inlaid ibis-headed guardians populate
the high-ceiling rooms. Glass cases of carved obsidian and jade
are all filled and labelled.

Besides themselves, eight men are waiting in the opulent surroundings that serve as the drawing room.

Each man is recognisable as a professional in his particular field and an expert in it. All learned scholars in one area or another regarding Egyptian history. They gather together, chatting like excited schoolboys, rarely meeting informally on mass like this except to attend award receptions, the odd ceremonial dinner, a trip to the seaside, or the Christmas Panto.

A few moments pass. A cold draft of air is felt around the room as footsteps approach along one of the corridors outside. The lighted candles in candelabras flicker; a few go out. The door handle turns, and a tall figure, a confident insect of a man, enters the room, and for an odd moment, he has the look of a clothed human praying mantis. He becomes the instant and expected centre of attention. Agile and fit, neither young nor old, wearing a colourful waistcoat and Prince of Wales check trousers. He flicks a gold fob watch from his waistcoat pocket and checks the time against a beautiful rosewood mantle clock before flashing a satisfied skull-like, drawn smile.

It is Singleton Sinclair.

'Good evening, gentlemen; thank you all for coming along this evening. It is bitterly cold outside, is it not? We may have cake later.' The attendant men perk up at this news. 'But before we do, I suppose you're all wondering why we should be gathered here tonight. Well, the short of it is this. Next week, Jonathan

Fern will be announcing the lucky fellow on whom he will generously bestow his award of sponsorship. He is a wealthy man, as I'm sure you are aware indeed, I am myself. He is also an old man; age is something we both have in common. I will be blunt, but what I'm about to propose, may grate against your moral standards, but maybe not. It is neither dishonest nor harmful to anyone. It is possibly benign in the extreme. I, unlike Fern, have no other heir when I shuffle off this mortal coil. Fern's amassed worldly collection will be inherited by his lovely daughter, who will no doubt dissolve his life's work to fund her many questionable charitable ventures.

'Do you think we will have ginger beer with the cake?' Rankin whispers to his friend as Singleton holds the floor.

'Shush... '

'I, on the other hand, have no one. My collection needs a home. It needs someone, a curator, such as one of you men here. I would, in turn, grant you full and unfettered title to the collected antiquities you are at present surrounded by. I would be your benefactor, a very generous benefactor at that. Should any of you prefer to place an allegiance with me?'
'What about your daughter?' someone asks. The question irritates Sinclair.

'We barely speak; she has no interest in my affairs nor I in hers.'

The men look around the room. Each casting glances around the walls at the priceless antiquities on display. There are many things to hold their attention. You can almost hear the wheels turning as the men weigh up Sinclair's coming proposal.

'To show you I mean what I say, the sum of five thousand pounds would be made available for him or, all of you to do as you wish by the end of the working day. The money can be available as early as the day after this meeting... tomorrow. With the added knowledge that in a very short time, all this would be yours. My bankers would issue a draft on my say-so, almost immediately.' He gestures around the room with a frail sweep of his arm and coughs, adding feebly, 'I'm not a well man.' He labours to the point as one of the attendant men speaks up.

'What do you mean an allegiance with you?' The lone voice is that of Professor Joseph. 'Of course, there is no man here that couldn't use that kind of money; it's more than most of us could possibly earn in a lifetime of lecturing on the university circuit or speaking in our capacity as professors and experts. University professorship is not a highly paid vocation, as I'm sure you know well.'

'I have heard rumours as such,' looking particularly frail, he slumps at the shoulders and then smiles. 'All I need from you is an undertaking that you will hold any information you may discover on the Fern-sponsored expedition until I can be notified. Nothing more, you will then receive the money. The expedition will go ahead in his name, but you will discover nothing.'

'Really, I know the rivalry between you two runs deep, but isn't this going a little too far?'
'Is it?' Sinclair sneers.
'I, for one, will not be a party to it.' The dissenter is Professor Hackett in his tweet jacket, 'and Sinclair's shifty scheme, well, he just won't back it!'
Sinclair drops the pretence of a smile. 'Ah, Professor, let me see, your deanship at Saint Mary's College pays you a princely sum of £162 a year, is that correct?' 'Yes... how could you know that?'
'I know a lot about each man here, far more than you might imagine, Professor Hackett. Including your Thursday night... excursions.' Professor Hackett reddens and nervously adjusts his collar as he rethinks his objection.

Sinclair points to an inlaid marble mantlepiece, on the top of which are nine crisp white sealed envelopes.

There are murmurings amongst the attendees... someone mentions cake again.

'Each of those envelopes contains five hundred pounds,
Sterling.' All the men's eyes widen in unison as they gaze upon
the envelopes before them. 'Only one of you receives the
sponsorship, so only one of you gets the acclaim, and then, only
then, if you find anything.' He pauses, gauging the men's
reaction.

So far, he is very pleased with what he sees. For most of his life,
he has bought what he wanted and cheated and bargained for
what he could not. Whatever method he took, he always got
what he wanted. At this point in his life, he wanted the souls of
these men around him and they would give them willingly.

'The rest of you will go back to your schools and colleges,
your... secrets, et cetera. Your meagre livings. I will offer you
five thousand pounds, a lifetime's wages in one night, and the
winner of the award will be the owner of my esteemed collection
when I am gone. All this for doing... nothing.' He lets the word
nothing hang in the air before continuing.
'Nothing more than just accepting my proposal. I leave you to
think about it, along with your... secrets, maybe?'

He smiles feebly, then almost limps from the room. It is Rankin
who speaks first.

'So, it seems some of us may be under threat of blackmail, too. I suppose each of us here has something that he would prefer the world did not know about.'
'We have been placed in a rather awkward situation, we also know each of us here has been selected for the chance of good fortune, but only one. Sinclair's proposal makes all of us rich men and still retains the claim of any discovery. No matter whose name is on the expedition.' The men all nod in agreement.

The consensus of opinion is in alignment with Rankin, after far less deliberated pontification than Singleton Sinclair had anticipated. He grins that the acceptance of his plan is so easily forthcoming as he listens from where he has secreted himself behind a large gilded statue of Horus and a small goat in a boat with a red coat. He begins to gloat.

****

We resume the conversation back at the house the following week, as it is relayed by Elizabeth Fern. Hackney and Littleton are spellbound, although for different reasons. Both stand transfixed by the words being spoken from those perfectly painted red lips.

They listen intently.

'What Singleton didn't know is that his maidservant, Kitty, and our maidservant, Molly, are very close friends. Kitty's passion for eavesdropping enabled Molly, who equally has a passion for rumour, to acquire the rather interesting story of Sinclair's plan as laid out at his dinner party.'

Elizabeth lights another cigarette and stares intently into the fire. Lord Fern breaks wind softly in the background.

'So, you see, it was me who specifically requested you to be here tonight. Yes, and it was I that rigged the papers for you to win. No one ever expects a rigged election. I want you to lead the expedition for my father and for me. You have it in you to become great men of history and leaders of expeditions so exciting and so wondrous that the world will be transfixed by them and your heroism.'

Both men are now under her spell, bull-shit though it may be. 'The exposure in your newspaper to highlight your reports will have a great impact. People will read each instalment with awe. Your public will follow you, and they will love you. Gentlemen, you will lead the expedition to find the lost Chantress of Asante. You will live on decades from now in everyone's minds, now and forever!'

The cuckoo clock chimes.

Her excitement is infecting the two reporters, who by now are harbouring illusions of impossible grandeur as great explorers and leaders of discoveries of many ancient buried things.

'Let us drink a toast to your success!'

Her passion awakens a misplaced confidence way beyond their abilities. She places three large glasses of sherry in front of them. Shadows flicker around the oak wood-paneled room. Despite her intimidating size, there was something beguiling, almost hypnotic about Elizabeth, and Littleton and Hackney were definitely under her spell.

'Your passage is booked on the next available steamer; you must make haste,' she draws closer. Both men can scarcely draw a breath. 'There is, of course, another who would outdo you and stop at nothing to make this his greatest acquisition. He was the bony, cantankerous cog here tonight.'
'Sinclair?' Both men repeat the name in unison. She nods.
'Yes, the man whose collection of funny-shaped, mummified camel dung is second only to my father's. Sinclair.' Her face suddenly changes as she spits his name into the fire, gazing almost madly into the shiny wine glass she is squeezing so

tightly, that it shatters between her vice-like gripping fingers. Elizabeth hardly notices. Littleton and Hackney draw closer to each other, seeing a strange intangible mystique to the woman they have just met, and the oddness of the last few hours. They contemplate their new situation, both wide-eyed, alert, and tingling with tension. Both were apprehensive, neither having a clue what they were getting themselves in for. The noise of the breaking glass brings them all back to reality, including Lord Fern.

Lord Fern, now awake again, struggles with a particularly heavy bout of flatulence and then amuses himself greatly by asking no one in particular, 'Who's cooking a cabbage?'

Littleton speaks first.

'I think, Miss Fern, you can safely rely on us to keep the world informed of our progress, and it will be nothing if not successful. Of course, we will need some help organising the expedition and maybe a crash course on Egyptology and what to do.'
'I don't suppose you have any vanilla fancies?' enquires Hackney.
'And tent pegs,' adds Littleton.
'Don't worry about a thing; it's all taken care of. It will not be an easy task; your journey may be long and fraught with many dangers, but you will be paid handsomely £5,000 pounds now and £5,000 on the successful discovery of your goal.'

Both men hit the ground at precisely the same time, blackness induced by money, a powerful incentive to an impromptu fainting spell. The two reporters, who moments before were fired and about to join the ranks of the soup kitchens' unemployed. Recovery is almost instant, as they pick themselves up from the floor. They will need tickets, and maps, and buckets, and scraping-digging-trowel equipment and tent pegs.

'Don't tell anyone when you are to depart, and speak to no one about our plans, or what I have told you. There is a special purpose to your appointment. One more thing, take this map as you will need it. It gives all the details. Carry it with you always. Let no one know you have it. Show it to no one; you cannot even tell your employer, Mister Jameson. I will sort it all out and notify him of events. You leave tonight; you will be informed of all further details in the morning; now make haste; everything will be all right, trust me. Good evening, gentlemen.' The door closes behind her. Then opens again.
'You will have your tent pegs...... and beware of the moon,' she says mysteriously and is gone.

She leaves the two men to contemplate her words as Lord Fern struggles with a protracted and particularly severe bout of his uncontrolled wind, that may or may not require the attention of a nurse and a warm, damp flannel.

'No cake then?' Hackney says with a slight tinge of disappointment in his voice as he and Littleton contemplate the adventure that lies ahead.

Chapter Four

The Voyage

The evening of the next day, Littleton and Hackney stand at the Southampton dockside. The sun has set and the chilly evening is well underway.

A bustling hive of productive activity is a very foreign place for the two men. Both of whom can only smile at their change in fortune. They have two one-way tickets and an assortment of trowels, brushes, spades, and buckets, tent pegs, too. All was supplied by Elizabeth before they departed for the port. All of which are now safely stowed away on board.

The newly minted explorers stand beneath the rusting port bow of an aged single-funnel steamer. The cracked, faded letters above her anchor chain spell out the name, 'The Doria.' She is of the intermediate class of workhorse steamship, at around 35,000 gross tonnage, run by the Green Star Line out of Liverpool. Worn wooden planking is bathed in the glow of the many gas lamps illuminating the waterside.

The port is teeming with life, even at this late hour, it being almost a quarter to midnight. Boxes of goods and freight are loaded noisily with pulleys and winches, all destined for global trade. Crates of supplies and equipment cradled in large, heavy rope nets are hoisted aboard the steamer. Thick smoke hangs heavily in the air from the diesel-engine cranes, along with the smell of cabbage or similar vegetables that vigorously assaults the nostrils.

A large brown rat, that had been unnervingly holding eye contact with Hackney, whilst nibbling on an indiscernible morsel, relinquishes its gaze and scampers off between some boxes and wooden crates - much to the relief of the two men who have dressed for the adventure ahead and eagerly await passenger boarding. 'Funny smell of cabbage, Hackney.' 'Indeed,' replied Hackney, sniffing. 'It is cabbages, isn't it?' Both men look around as if the question was never asked.
'Old man Jameson never expected this. Here we are bound for Egypt to report on our very own expedition.' Both men giggle at their words. The very notion would have been a dream twenty-four hours ago.

'What a turnaround. I'd love to have been a fly on the wall when Miss Fern told him. I bet anyone's mouth never opened so wide; the look on the old man's face would have been priceless. Three days ago, we were considered unknown and incompetent in the world of Egyptology. Now, we are feted as true expedition leaders. Hackney, old chum, we are the news! My auntie would be so proud.' Hackney can do nothing but beam with a schoolboy's enthusiastic grin at his new predicament.

He rolls one of his Everlasting Bullseye gobstoppers from cheek to cheek.

'Hackney, old friend, it's our job to show him what we are really made of. But you do have a point; given our knowledge of the ancient kingdoms is less than precise, we are not the obvious choice to lead such an expedition. There's something a little strange about all this. Elizabeth Fern is a mysterious woman, all right. She has arranged everything to the letter for this trip, and everything seems to fit perfectly... except for you and me.' Littleton ponders.

A foghorn sounds off in the distance.

Hackney frowns then coughs hard, spitting his gobstopper out with alarming velocity, startling Littleton's preoccupation with their suitability for the mission. It bounces along the planking a few yards before. Quick as a flash, the scruffy brown rat has it in its claws before scampering from view between two old, damp, wooden barrels.

'Will you stop doing that?' Littleton catches his breath, punching in the area of his heart. Hackney's cause for concern then becomes apparent. Wide-eyed and pointing to a pallet in the distance, he brings his friend's attention to some luggage being loaded onto the ship.

'Look over there at those bags and cases, they have the mark, the mark of the... black scarab.'

'Singleton Sinclair's signature, he must be on the boat as well.'
'What shall we do?' Hackney clutches Littleton's arm.
'That's his mark, all right. I'll wager you are right; those are his luggage cases; we must be on our most astute guard. It's a good thing we are a pretty shrewd pair when it comes down to it.'
'Yes, we'll take no piffle,' asserts Hackney.
Another foghorn sounds flat and long in the distance.

The morning air is fresh and salty; the Doria has been underway all night. A steady headwind whistles as it buffets around the radio lines and the ocean foams at the dipping bow wake. Littleton and Hackney awake to the sound of the many white gulls trailing the ship.

Hackney leaves the top bunk with a zest and vitality, believing he has mariner's blood coursing through his veins this morning. He lands, placing one foot securely in the chamber pot that Littleton has been making use of for the better part of the night.

After cleaning up and dressing, Hackney informs Littleton that he will find them both some breakfast and get something for Littleton's seasickness. Littleton's only response is: 'I wish I were dead.'

Ten minutes later, Hackney returns to the cabin, chewing a piece of toast and grinning like a Cheshire Cat.

'Look, Littleton, we made yesterday's papers! I got this copy of the Times from one of the other passengers; they had finished with it anyways.' Littleton was now out of bed half-dressed and sitting above the commode again, awaiting nature's course with just a towel covering his modesty, looking very sorry for himself. 'Even managed to pick up some sherbet dabs from the concierge,' he offers one to Littleton from his small paper bag.

'Oh, don't knock, never mind me,' he snatches the paper from his friend.
'Where's the piece about us?' Hackney points, smiling to a smaller article headed in capitals.

REPORTERS TO LEAD EXPEDITION.

'Journalist Harry Hackney and his assistant Larry Littleworth?' Littleton chokes on the word 'assistant' and the misspelling of his own name and repeats it with disbelief.

Hackney turns and adjusts his collar whilst staring out of the porthole.

'I think they must have misunderstood what I said,' Hackney says not too convincingly, rather sheepishly, not directly looking at Littleton.
'I didn't say anything.' He jabs his finger into the air to make

the point. Littleton continues as the printed put-down only adds to his nausea. He continues reading aloud.

'...his assistant Larry Littleworth,' he pauses again at the misspelling of his name and sighs heavily before continuing.

'The two men have pulled off what can only be described as the coup of the century. The two 'A History Weekly' journalists received the sponsorship for the Lord Fern Expedition and are set to depart for Egypt on Friday. Many eminently qualified candidates were rumoured to be favoured, but the two lads from Bermondsey, London, pipped them to the post. The fabled high Chantress of Asante has been sought by many. And many a man has been lost doing so, men never to be heard from again, the last being Dr. Ernest Saunders, founder of the Great Cracker Empire, Saunders Savoury Snacks. As reported in this paper about his mysterious disappearance five years ago. Nothing of the terrible curse and evil prophecy seems to have dampened these two lads' ardour, and we wish them well. In the words of Dr Hackney, he quoted, 'History depends on the availability of written records; we are the men to provide them.' Good luck, boys, we wish you well and hope that you may return - if possible - alive.'

From behind the open newspaper, nature can be heard taking its course as Littleton's bowels get to grips with what he has just read. He looks at Hackney.

'So, you are a doctor now? Say, doc, may I call you doc?'
Littleton sarcastically addresses Hackney. 'You didn't speak to
anyone, did you 'doc' before our departure then?' A sheepish
smile is all Hackney can do as he sniffs the air.
'I can smell those cabbages again,' the two men stare at each
other.
'Aside from my demotion to your assistant, and your PhD.
There are a couple of troubling points in this article.' 'Yes, fancy
them spelling your name wrong like that?' Hackney responds.
'You didn't notice anything about a curse and horrible death?'
'Well, I did, but it's something of a cliche with these trips to
Egypt. It comes with the territory, so to speak; it adds spice to
the story,' Hackney replies unconcerned, then adds. 'Tommy-
rot, I'd say- pure poppycock.'
'What about this Saunders fellow then?' Littleton says, pointing
back to the article.
'Never heard of him,' dismisses Hackney as he finishes his last
mouthful of toast.

****

75

FIVE YEARS EARLIER

We travel five years back to a small archaeological expedition going on beneath the blistering sun somewhere in the hot, arid Watabe Desert. Turbaned native porters, in peasant garb, brush and sieve sand through coarse wire metal sieves. While others remove the barrows of debris, the encampment is a bustling hive of activity.

Inside one of the heavy cotton tents, two men talk and study a recently unearthed artefact. One of the men is Dr. Ernest Saunders; he is examining some faint markings on the stone with a large magnifying glass. Saunders has a set of thick mutton chop whiskers parted beneath his chin. The second man is a young bearded native, by the name of Bengay-Wat. He is dressed also in the cool native garb, like almost all the men labouring outside. A simple linen turban helps cover Bengay's dark, swarthy features, contrasting strikingly with the pale, jolly, white-haired man beside him.

He and Dr. Saunders are engrossed (and excited) about the faint inscriptions on the stone. Saunders has his glasses raised on his forehead. Both crouch above the rock on the table. The rock looks to be only one-half of the original artefact.

'Bengay, we are on the brink of a great discovery, my friend,' he points to a rudimentary map scribed on the stone's surface. 'This is almost the position of where we are now digging. We are close, so very close.'

Bengay is agitated; he licks his lips, and whatever soothing effect Saunders' words were intended to have is not forthcoming.

'You say that every day, and every day, we find nothing. We have only uncovered an empty chamber, and that is all - a septic tank from the royal latrines, you say. We will now need to be paid; we cannot search forever. I am as excited as you about this, but please give me the money to pay my men.'
'I know the men need payment; I am all too aware. I shall be honest with you, Bengay. I am penniless at the moment. My last trip to the Oasis Club on Saturday night and those brief few hours with Tamara ... ' His eyes gleam as he speaks her name. 'She cost me my last guinea. I know you will understand, for you have sampled her charms on occasion, and who could resist?'

He smiles at Bengay, who is not smiling back but giving all the signs that he may be about to explode.

'You look very annoyed; don't do something you may regret.'
Saunders realises too late that his companion is very, very
upset. Bengay makes toward the cowering Dr. Saunders,
holding the heavy flat stone above his head. He has an odd limp
that causes him almost to stagger and lurch.

'Don't misunderstand me; you and your men will be paid when
we discover the Chantress. We shall all be rich men.' The
calming effect that these words were supposed to have on
Bengay again was a futile endeavour. Saunders tries to smile as
Bengay brings down the half stone and makes it into two-

quarters across the doctor's head. The 1907 Saunders expedition ended that day.

The rest of the men broke camp and every clue that they were ever there was erased. Except that is for the good doctor, who was left clubbed unconscious and entombed inside his only discovery of the last few weeks. The royal septic tank chamber, being resealed and covered over, now with him inside it. Along with the latrine, his fate was sealed, or so it was thought.

****

PRESENT DAY 1912

Back on board the Doria. Littleton and Hackney stroll along the promenade deck trying to climatise themselves to the new situation. The breakfast and morning stroll, along with the passage of a few hours, has calmed Littleton's sea sickness and he has recovered somewhat.

'If Singleton Sinclair is aboard this ship, it won't be long before we meet him. I don't think the Doria is fully booked; there can't be that many passengers, and we are bound to spot him. He has to come out sometime.' Hackney produces a small publication on Egyptology from his overcoat, 'We need to brush up on our knowledge of all things Ancient and Egyptian.'

'Yes, good idea, we should take every opportunity to test one another. We need to cloak the bones of our limited knowledge with at least the semblance of a rudimentary understanding of our quest and quarry.' Littleton waxes lyrically.

'Er quite... I have this pamphlet; it is very informative. I'll flip through the pages to find a question with which to test you. Knowledge is power and all that,' Hackney quips. But a pained expression crosses his face as he flicks from page to page, unable to find or understand a pertinent question.

Dejectedly, they both lean against the handrail and look out over the dark, black ocean travelling forty feet beneath them. Hackney suddenly raises the pamphlet to cover his face, agitatedly speaking in whispered tones from behind the pages. Only his eyes are visible above the open pamphlet under the brim of his hat.

'Don't turn around. It's him, it's Sinclair.' Hackney nods in a gesture to somewhere behind Littleton. Littleton remains rigid but calm; he does not look around.
'Are you sure?' he asks between clenched teeth. Hackney nods discreetly in the affirmative. Littleton takes a few steps back then, without warning, spins around his cape, fluttering as he pirouettes within a few feet of the tall gentleman who has his back to them.

'Ah, Mr. Sinclair, what a pleasure,' tapping the man on his shoulder. This is all he manages to say, as if by some strange and unforeseen quirk of fateful coincidence, from seemingly nowhere, a large black-backed seagull strikes him squarely in the back of the head, propelling him as if by some invisible hand. Littleton crashes headfirst onto the deck. Both Littleton and the bird, just as before, now lay unconscious on the deck planking.

A crowd instantly gathers around the felled passenger and his seabird. Hackney stoops, picking up the bird that is clutching a small herring in its webbed feet. The limp bird, drops the fish, which disappears unnoticed into Littleton's clothing as Hackney holds up the bird for closer inspection. The crowd is seemingly more interested in the bird than in the unconscious Littleton. The fellow, whom they believe to be Singleton Sinclair, turns around. It is not him, but a similarly built, gangly gentleman. He disappears in the commotion and melts into the crowd. A white-vested steward appears and approaches them to help with the passenger, who appears to have fainted.

'It must be an ornithological anomaly,' Hackney exclaims, holding the bird by its limp neck.

'Talk about lightning striking twice?' He cradles the bird, holding the gull, lifting its beak, as if throwing a paper dart. The ship's speed and undiscernible headwind cause its wings to assume the position of flight, whereupon he gently launches the gull into the wind to the steward's amazement.

They both watch it soar away on the gusting air current with several other amazed fellow passengers.

'You can't half-fly those anomalies, sir.' They both stare, watching the gull become a small, indistinguishable dot on the horizon.
'Something I learned as a boy, let's get my companion here inside. I don't think the briskness of the sea air and local birdlife agree with him.' They shoulder Littleton's dead weight together, making their way into the passenger lounge, which is a lot warmer.

Hackney takes stock of his surroundings; he is pleasantly surprised. It is not grand but civilised, and there are far more passengers than he had initially been aware of. He surmises that the Doria makes as much out of fare-paying passengers as it does out of the shipment of cargo freight.

There were waiters and stewards to administer to the passengers' whims, and the standard of the decor would do justice to a fully fitted white star liner.

Elizabeth had chosen their transport well. This was indeed a much better ship than he had first imagined. Some concerned women leave their card game and come over to help. Other people merely looked on with curiosity and mild surprise.

Littleton was placed in a vacant, finely upholstered wingback chair while Hackney and the steward sauntered over to the bar area, where Hackney regaled those interested in the erroneous flight of the gull into his friend. The seagull and its meeting with Littleton's cranium were to be talked about for days. He also mentioned that a similar experience had occurred with an owl a few days before sailing had commenced - much to everyone's shocked disbelief.

As things normalised, an ear-piercing rather lady-like scream was heard (again) long and loud from the centre of the small crowd that was still assembled around Littleton. A flash of silver, not dissimilar to a herring, leaps from within his clothing, flying high in the direction of the bar before landing on the marbled bar top, flapping once. Then, bouncing into the heavily fruited cocktail of an attractive and strikingly attired woman, sitting alone beneath the shadow of a large brimmed hat at the end of the bar. Her legs were covered by the long pleats of a dark, velvet skirt draped over the tall stool and her arms swathed by the fine silks of a perfectly tailored jacket. She looked like a woman whose upkeep would be beyond most men's means.

At this point, the fish had spent too much time away from its natural habitat, and now, coupled with its airborne adventure (and its present emersion in a banana daiquiri), it was looking less than well. Everyone at the bar witnessed its expiration. Hackney calmly walks to where the lady is sitting. He flashes a smile, then removes the fish by its tail as if it were a job he did every day, introducing himself to her with a suave flourish. 'How do you do, Miss; may I relieve you of this naughty stowaway?' Taking the fish by its tail, he puts it into his inside pocket as if it were a cigar or a fountain pen. Almost immediately, he's very taken and disarmed by this beautiful flaxen-haired beauty before him. Smiling a particularly pasty smile, Hackney engages in his one-sided conversation.

'May I offer you a little confectionary: a Gobstopper perhaps?' he produces his crumpled brown paper bag from his pocket and sits down beside her. His attention, and everyone else's, is solely focused on the attractive woman dressed in her flowing, rich velvets and satins. Disdainfully, she waves away his offered confectionery.

'No, thank you. I was enjoying my drink alone,' she
says tartly. He doesn't notice or skip a beat. He has fallen for
her, beguiled by the looks of an angel. He puts his brown bag
away.
'I'm sorry, how rude of me, allow me to get you another drink.'
Gesturing towards the barman.
'Another drink for the lady, if you please, and I'll take a small
beer, why not?' he reveals a more confident side to his
personality as he becomes the pursuer of this young lady's
heart. No amount of rebuttal can penetrate his thick hide once
so engaged.
'I'm travelling with my companion,' he gestures without looking
to where he left Littleton. 'We are going on an expedition,' he
says proudly.
'Really?'
'Yes, really. In fact, I am leading it,' he says fancifully. He
doesn't read the sarcasm and the snide intonation in her voice.

Instead, he leans back on his stool, trying to look as refined and
important an expedition leader as he can to this very attractive
young woman. 'You might have read about it in the papers. I
say, you must think me terribly rude, but we haven't been
introduced. My name is Harry Hackney.' Offering her his hand,
but she merely smiles.

'Not The Harry Hackney?' feigning admiration. He looks
around the room, 'Indeed, I am he.'
She nods, seemingly more interested, 'Tell me more.'

'Yes, the very same. You have read about us in the newspapers,
then?'

'The famous explorer...Well, it is an honour. My name is Sonia,
Sonia Sinclair.' She takes a small business card from her purse
and hands it to Hackney. He does not notice the scarab
signature embossed upon it as he takes it from her and places it
in his pocket.

'I wish we could talk more, but I'm very busy. Now, if you excuse me, I have some reading to do.'

With that, she gets up from the bar and is gone. Hackney leans back on his chair and sighs at her disappearing vision as she makes her way out of the bar. He fails to recognise the significance of her name. Which has completely alluded him, he is aware only of her rose-scented perfume and beguiling hazel eyes, a dream. The abruptness of her departure is no issue.

'Odds Bodkins, I say... ' he speaks to himself as no-one is near to hear him.

Meanwhile, Littleton has come to and is sitting upright, wide-eyed, a rather startled expression on his face as a kind old lady pats his wrist. He wonders why a wet fish should leap from his clothing while a crowd of onlookers surrounds him.

Moments later, Littleton approaches the bar unsteadily, rubs the back of his head, and sits down. Hackney doesn't notice he is still staring after Sonia, beguiled. His heart was once again pierced by Cupid's arrow.

'The old dear just told me what happened,' says Littleton as he sits down beside Hackney. 'If another bird flies into me again...'

The words don't come easily, and as the frustration bubbles, he sighs and shakes his head. 'What was it this time?'

'Oh, a large seagull with a fish, a black-back gull actually, a rather handsome fellow in winter plumage.' He's reminded that he still has the fish and reaches into his coat pocket, handing it to Littleton - still not wholly thinking straight. His mind is occupied with his latest infatuation.

Littleton eyes the fish and now has something to focus his frustration on. He takes it from Hackney and holds it up in front of him as if it will listen as he speaks to the herring. 'They see me as some sort of suicide beacon. I mean, what are the chances of that? So that's twice in as many days; my head won't take much more of this Hackney.'

Hackney has now rejoined his friend here on planet Earth and is listening, although less than intently, as Littleton vents his frustrations towards the fish. Slowly, his rage subsides, and he realises where he is and what he is holding. He scowls one last time contemptuously at the herring before tossing it, defeated, over his shoulder, where it bounces behind the bar.

'I need a drink,' exhausted he calls over the barman. The bow-tied and waistcoated barman approaches smiling. The smile turns to open-mouthed surprise. The correctly positioned barman meets with the incorrectly placed shiny, slippery fish. Both his legs appear to be heading for the ceiling and, thereafter, a brief pause, back towards the floor with equal momentum. Landing with a distinct dull thud behind the bar. Hackney looks over the bar at the crushed remains of the herring and the prostrate barman. Both men consider that the placing of the fish in the barman's path may have played a small part in his present position.
'Maybe we should get cabin service?'
'Good idea.' Both men retreat at speed from the bar back to the cabin.

Back in the cabin, the two journalists take stock of the situation. Hackney paints a picture of Sonia Sinclair's beauty and her beautiful eyes, whilst passing the card that she gave him. Littleton sits bolt upright as he reads the name embossed on the card.

'Wait a minute, did you say Sinclair? You fool, that's his daughter; those were her bags being loaded aboard at Southampton. It even has a beetle on it.'

There is a loud knock on the cabin door. 'Who is it?' asks Littleton.

'Steward, sir.'

'Stewart, who?' asks Hackney.

'No sir, Steward, cabin services you ordered.' They both are aware that neither man had time to order anything. Both mouth the question silently to one another and shake their heads. 'We will play along,' Hackney says quietly shielding his voice with his hand. 'Oh, just leave it outside, will you?'

'Very good sir.'

Without thinking, but by way of adding a legitimate reason for him having to do so, Hackney adds, 'We're naked.'

Then, realising its implications and how the remark might be interpreted, he adds quickly, 'We had a shower separately, not together. I'm dressed,' he digs himself deeper and squirms, biting hard on his fist as Littleton grimaces in disbelief. 'Whatever you say, sir, whenever you finish, it's outside the door.' The voice recedes as he walks away from the cabin. 'Well done, Hackney, I couldn't have put it better myself.'

They tiptoe for no apparent reason to the cabin door, waiting a moment before opening it a fraction. There is no one there. The corridor is empty save for a silver-covered dining tray.

They slowly open the door more fully. 'Perhaps we're being overly cautious,' Hackney smiles, removing the lid expectantly. He is met by the gaze of a large death-head Cobra, that now faces them wide-eyed with a licking hiss and flicking forked tongue. Both men hold the cobra's gaze. Its flattened head is suspended by an invisible thread pulled by an unseen puppeteer. The snake hisses loudly as it tastes the air.

Great Scott! It's a snake!' gasps
Hackney.

'I know that! Neither of us ordered
a snake, did we?' Hackney shakes
his head quickly, slamming down the
lid plate, then shutting the door.
The fiendish, hissing, green grin was now behind an inch of solid mahogany. After a moment of gathering his thoughts, Littleton speaks.

'Right, someone is out to get us. What did you say to that woman, Sonia Sinclair? What did you say, Harry... think?' Hackney ponders a moment on the question.

'Nothing. We hardly spoke at all. I can't believe she would be responsible for this,' he gestures towards the door. 'A man-eating snake outside our door, who would do such a thing? Besides, the steward's voice was a man's, not a woman's.'

'It doesn't eat you; it bites you. It is poisonous. At best, it could give you a nasty suck.' He opens the door just a crack to see the venomous delivery has now disappeared.
'Quick, look, it's gone, the snake and the tray.'
'I've got a feeling someone doesn't want us to find a certain lost High Chantress. Why would Sinclair send his daughter to follow us and why would she send a snake to our cabin to bite us?'

Littleton sits on the bottom bunk, frowning. Hackney awaits Littleton's opinion as he has grown accustomed to deferring to his friend's thoughts. As he listens, he opens one of the three cabin portholes with its large brass thumb screws. The salty smell of the sea air reminds Littleton of his seasickness.

'All of this is very strange, perhaps; it would be a good idea for you to get to know this, Sonia Sinclair.'

'I'll say!' Hackney smiles with unbridled enthusiasm. 'There is something fishy here and I don't mean... the fish.'

'What, do you think her intentions less-than-honorable? Look, she very probably has nothing to do with any of this, and you are imagining forces against us, demons where there are none.' 'Did I just imagine that snake then? Did I just imagine it disappeared? I did not.'

Littleton is adamant. Hackney leans against the dresser, feeling the airflow from the open porthole; what he does not feel is the long hairy fingers of a large female arachnid alight on his jacket. A giant tarantula: the slow creeping of its hairy fingers

makes their way over the tweed of his clothing. Littleton glances up, noticing the spider, and is frozen. The spider is crawling delicately along Hackney's supporting arm.

Calmly, Hackney takes stock of the situation. As he rolls the aniseed ball he has been sucking on quickly around his mouth, before taking careful aim. A look of extreme concentration envelopes his features. He then fills his cheeks before blowing hard and causing the small rock-like ball of sugar to be expelled from between his lips like a bullet. It strikes the insect with such velocity as to knock it completely across the cabin into Littleton's half-covered chamber pot with a sickening splashing plop.

'Good heavens, where did you learn to do that?' Littleton asks as he throws a towel over the pot.
'As a boy, old chap.'
'Do you suppose that was a coincidence, too? If he has any friends, we don't want to meet them?' Hackney gingerly approaches the chamber pot, lifting the towel, and looks in. 'He was a particularly ugly-looking fellow, all his legs have fallen off by the look of him.'
Littleton joins him, frowning, looking over Hackney's shoulder into the pot.
'That is not the spider.'

'Somebody is out to get us, Hackney. I brought along some
books. I'll look up more info on our quarry, the High
Chantress. A little background knowledge could go a long way
and I think maybe you should get on more friendly terms with
our Miss Sinclair as soon as possible.' Hackney smiles at the
suggestion, 'I'll turn on the charm as best I can.'
'You know, I always admire the way you are able to charm the
ladies, Hackney. If there is one thing you do well, it's put
women at ease. Don't ask me how, but it would not be unfair to
say you are cat-nip to the fairer sex. I'll meet you in the bar in
an hour.'
'What if she's not there?' Hackney pauses.
'Oh, I have a feeling she will be there all right. What would be a
better alibi?' Hackney raises an eyebrow in agreement, 'To the
bar.' He closes the cabin door behind him.

The bar is busier than at lunchtime. People are dressed for
dinner and awaiting their seating in the dining room. Some
stand casually chatting with others at various tables. At one
such secluded table, all but obscured by a large potted palm sits
Miss Sonia Sinclair. She is alone reading a book.

'Mind if I join you?' Hackney the pursuer sits down, once again,
uninvited. His smile is not returned, indeed her eyes blaze,
almost startled by his unexpected appearance.

She quickly regains her composure and even manages a half-hearted contortion of her lips, uttering a pleasant 'Not at all,' that could almost pass as a smile.

Hackney pulls up a chair.
'Oh, doctor, we meet again, yes, of course.' Hackney is once again beguiled by her vision. Could she possibly be the owner of a poisonous snake and a hairy spider?

Meanwhile back in the cabin, surrounded by books that he has pulled from a large leather travel case, Littleton is fast asleep. He is having his own dreams about another Sinclair.

The warmth of the cabin and his weariness have soon induced a heavy slumber, curtailing his study and he lies full length on his bunk. Ancient gods parade past him, hawk and jackal-headed, unseen, but for a moment in the darkness. Passages from the books repeat themselves. A dog-headed God and the vile serpent. A banana on a stick. The hissing slithering snake was now laughing with the head of Singleton Sinclair!

He awakes startled and sweating. The few moments of slumber have seemed like hours. He quickly dresses for dinner, relieved it is just a dream, and leaves the confines of the cabin.

In the bar, Littleton spots Hackney sitting with Sonia Sinclair at the small table. They're deep in conversation, or rather, Hackney is. Littleton skirts around the room, trying to get a measure of the woman, who, as Hackney has already described, is disarmingly attractive. Aside from a slight collision with a waiter, coupled with the sound of shattering glass, his presence in the bar goes unnoticed.

He approaches the two nonchalantly.

'Hello, Hackney. I didn't know you were here. Who is your friend?' Littleton asks, smiling at Sonia. Both turn to Littleton, as he stands - there is only seating for two at the table. 'I'm Lawrence Littleton, editor-in-chief of 'A History Weekly', how do you do?' Holding his hand towards her, Sonia Sinclair keeps her hands firmly at her side and returns his greeting with a nod, casting an icy glance at Hackney.

'Sonia Sinclair, I believe you have met my father.' 'Not Singleton Sinclair - the eminent Egyptologist's daughter?' he inquires as if surprised.
'I think you know very well who I am.' 'Yes, well er... '
There is an awkward silence.
'Well, gentlemen, I have had quite enough of your company for one day, in fact quite enough of your company, well... forever and certainly, this journey.'

Hackney is taken aback by her sudden bluntness. 'I say that's rather uncalled for.'

'Rather like your company,' she snarls. 'We will be in Alexandria in a few days, let's hope for all our sakes our paths do not cross for the remainder of the voyage.' She rises from her chair directing her gaze, mainly at Hackney, before jabbing him in the shoulder with her calf skin gloved finger. 'Especially you.'

Hackney straightens his tie nervously. 'You have told me all I need to know.' With that, she leaves both men, who nod politely at her departure. Hackney, a little wide-eyed and disappointed. Littleton was thoughtful and frowning. Hackney speaks first. 'Did she say snakes?'

'She said for all our sakes... ' Littleton shakes his head. 'Well, if that doesn't take the biscuit... You know you were right; there is a side to Miss Sinclair I hadn't seen.' Littleton fixes Hackney with a stare.

Littleton turns to Hackney, 'What did she mean? You have told her all she needed to know?'

Hackney shifts uncomfortably in his chair and stares at his nails. 'Well, I told her that we have gotten the sponsorship funding for the expedition from Lord Fern. Who knows how?

As we are not really experts in that field, Egypt and all that. I told her we had been working at 'A History Weekly' because I was Jameson's nephew. And because of our relations, nobody dared to sack us. We were probably a little lucky to be awarded the chance to look for the Chantress. But we were keen, and we were learning as quickly as possible. Then I mentioned Elizabeth Fern and how she managed to get Jameson to send us to the dinner that night, from which we won the lottery, and that we were just a couple of lucky eggs, really.'

'Anything else?'

'I wasn't a real doctor,' he pauses to meet Littleton's gaze. 'You didn't leave anything out then?'

'Well, I was the one doing all the talking,' he replies sheepishly.

Chapter Five
Mistaken Identity

The remainder of the voyage passed uneventfully, if somewhat anxiously, on the part of Littleton and Hackney.

It got warmer the farther south they travelled. Due to the unusually calm sea, Littleton experienced little more of the sea sickness that had initially plagued him.

Dinner was the social high point of the day. Lots of cake afterwards. Both of them became quite friendly with a retired army major and his wife, who sat at their table. The major shared stories of the many military campaigns he had been engaged in; he would display his various scars and wounds to validate any of his more exuberant adventures. Each of his tales further wetting the two men's appetite for the forthcoming travel and adventure that surely must lay ahead. The African campaigns he listed could have taken up two voyages. However, his story of single-handedly holding fifty fuzzy wuzzies at bay during the Crimea was just a little tinged with romantic embellishment.

The major's wife would listen stoically, doe-eyed, and enthralled by her husband as if she was hearing the stories for the first time.

Sonia Sinclair didn't show herself again, to Hackney's concealed disappointment. The days were spent catching up with the study of Egyptology, with the help of a few small books that Littleton had thought to bring along. 'I Spy Egyptology', a very primitive children's book, was the most informative. They did the best they could.

Hackney sent two telegrams and received one from Lady Fern, giving details and instructions about their disembarkation and arrival in Alexandria. Their contact in Alexandria was to be Farouk Akesh, a local curiosity shop dealer and amateur photographer who would make himself known to them on docking.

After skirting the African coast for a few days, the Doria steams into her berth at the port. The ship gradually slides along the dockside, and heavy rope hawsers are thrown to the men waiting on the key side. Once secured, both Littleton and Hackney scan the teeming terminal for their contact Farouk.

The air carries the heavy smell of spices, bagged and ready for shipping; dried fish and fruit in vast quantities line the key side. The disorganised jumble of the vivid colours is a sharp contrast to the grey Southampton they had left behind. Exotic screaming animals and caged birds are stacked, looking so alien to the Englishmen. The olive-skinned people of the port wore clothes and headdresses of many hues. Everyone was engaged in some activity. They said their goodbyes to the major and his wife, watching them melt away into the crowd, followed by many small street children in varying degrees of unwashed filthiness vying for a few tossed coins.

'Owee - I say Ooeee boys!'

A diminutive, small, dark man with a monkey on his shoulders was making his way toward them, waving and calling. He moved in the oddest drunken fashion. Staggering and smiling but waving at them. Littleton and Hackney turn to make sure that it was not someone else who was attracting this small, odd fellow's attention.

It wasn't.

Both waited uneasily for him to reach them.

'Look at you here already; the telegram was so vague,' he says between breaths. 'You must think me so disorganised, but we have had so much to do, and my friend here,' he gestures with a smile to the monkey, 'he has not been well.'

They both exchange a glance as the two men survey the ruffled appearance of the odd-looking stranger.

'Allow me to introduce myself. I am Farouk Akesh and this is my monkey, Minki.' He pats the monkey gently on the head and gives him a peanut.
'Hello, Minki,' Hackney smiles and greets the little monkey very naturally, almost as if he expects the cute macaque to answer him back.

Farouk Akesh is a lot shorter than both Littleton and Hackney. His monkey was coming in about their chin height, with dark olive skin, with a large bushy moustache, his slight frame supporting an old linen suit, and a particularly battered fez hat. The monkey wears a shiny, identical fez with a matching waistcoat. But the oddest thing about Farouk, that anybody couldn't fail to notice, was that he seemed to experience great difficulty keeping his balance.

The monkey acted as an extra pair of arms or counterbalance, either leaning out some or using something for support by throwing its weight in the opposite direction. Farouk looked as if he might fall if the monkey didn't keep his balance for him.

'Here, give Minki a peanut; he's recovering from a slight case of Icky Ticki,' he hands a few nuts to Littleton, who complies. Smiling weakly as he tries to show enthusiasm for this

impromptu monkey feeding session. 'What's Icky Ticki?' asks
Hackney.

Even though Minki hasn't finished his last peanut, he takes one
half-heartedly from Littleton and puts it in his mouth. Chewing
it slowly, then without warning, he burps and coughs violently
before quickly throwing up a javelin of projectile vomit onto
Littleton's outstretched arm and shoulder.

All three men stare at the warm monkey mess now steaming on
Littleton's sleeve.

'See, he is still not well, are you Minki? That is the Icky Ticki,'
Farouk says, taking a handkerchief from his jacket, and wiping
the edges of the monkey's mouth delicately before returning it
to his pockets as if nothing had happened.

Littleton is rigid with rage, he cannot speak. But glares at
Farouk, who only then realises the steaming pile of monkey
vomit on his new acquaintance's shoulder is causing him the
utmost displeasure. He fumbles in his pocket and again retrieves
the less-than-clean handkerchief. Littleton takes it, registers its
dampness, and inwardly squirms. He attends to the patch of
undigested monkey fluids on his clothing.

'Come, I have booked your rooms at the Wandering Camel; it was the best I could do at such short notice. Don't worry about your bags; I will have them picked up later. We have much to talk about; I have hired a team of diggers and excellent, trusted labour. First, we shall meet my nephew, a wonderful young apprentice. He knows all the good places to dig.' Smiling, he winks and taps his nose. His smile is bristling with uneven yellow teeth, with the exception of a lone prominent gold addition. A worrying smile passes between the two men.

'You both must be tired, so we will take refreshments when we reach the Camel.'

With that, the three men and the monkey, Minki set off from the shipside. Between the market stalls, traders try to sell anything they can. The beggars and street urchins descend like flies as soon as they are spotted. Merchants' stalls selling everything from carpets to candles, spices to soup bowls, through the hustle and bustle between donkeys and oxen, loaded with clanking pots and pans and other multicoloured household goods. A small group of grimy children are imitating Farouk as they trail behind them, but gradually tire and give up their amusing game as they make their way through the thinning crowd.

'Well, we're off on our adventure,' Hackney smiles. They slowly follow Farouk as he staggers lopsidedly ahead. Minki studies Littleton at every opportunity; Littleton merely glares at the stain on his shoulder. The hustle and bustle of the port area gives way to less crowded streets and alleys. Light pastel-coloured buildings on either side of the cooler-shaded alleyways. The enclosed cool valleys of the streets offer some respite from the heat of the day, being just wide enough to pull a cart through. All the time, Farouk's monkey keeps his balance for him every time he looks as though he may topple; it's his long-outstretched arms using the vertical walls to steady him.

After searching, for what seemed like a good fifteen minutes, with little or nothing being said in the labyrinth of alleyways and narrow streets, all looking very much the same at this point. The group stopped outside a rather dilapidated building, with paint-peeling closed shutters and a few overturned wooden crates outside.

Sweating profusely, Farouk pauses, wiping his forehead with his handkerchief. They all were feeling the dry, still, blistering heat, even in the shade of the dark alleys. Looking around, Farouk raises his hand, waving as if signaling to an unseen friend.

'This is the place, is it?' Hackney says, looking around,
frowning. Farouk also now looks around uneasily but manages
a gold-toothed weasel-like smile. Both men now begin to have
slight reservations about their new sweaty acquaintance and his
motives. They become acutely aware that they may have made
a mistake trusting him and his monkey so readily.

'I say, what's your game, Akesh? What are you up to?'
Littleton stammers. A leery grin crosses Farouk's
leathery cheeks and he begins to back away from the two men
towards the open end of the alleyway. The end of which now
has four shadowy figures advancing toward them. The other
end of the alley is no escape; they are trapped. The further end
of the alleyway got narrower until it reached a high wall. All the
potential doorways were boarded up. They were cornered like
rats in a drainpipe.

The shadowy figures became men, men whose intentions
Littleton and Hackney could only surmise, but they didn't look
like friendly natives curious to befriend the two foreigners. They
carried weapons, bludgeons, and coshes. They had been tricked
into an easy trap.

It was quickly becoming a tight situation.

As the prospective assailants advanced, their features became
clear, and so did their intentions.

Suddenly, Hackney lunged at Farouk, who covered his face instinctively. Hackney grabs Farouk's Monkey, Minki. Wrenching it from his shoulders with both hands, subduing its flailing arms. Its wild screaming broke the silence and echoed around the deserted alleyway.

The four men stopped and stared in disbelief before looking to Farouk for instructions. Farouk, wide-eyed and seething, was leaning against the wall, unable to keep his balance without his monkey, Minki. Hackney, meanwhile, was gripping his charge tightly and doing his best to restrain the screaming creature.

'One more move from you and the monkey gets it!'
'He's not bluffing,' says Littleton by way of support. He held the monkey tightly with both arms outstretched as if he were offering it to them.
'One step closer, and I'll smash his brains all over this wall; I've done it before.' If the monkey didn't speak English, he gave all the outward signs of understanding it. His wailing and struggling stopped; it was a standoff.
'Stop! Not my monkey, don't hurt my monkey. My Minki, please. I made a mistake, you gentlemen can go, only leave Minki he's a good monkey.' Farouk spoke with genuine desperation in his voice. 'Please.'

One of the four thugs spoke quickly to Farouk in a language that neither Littleton nor Hackney could understand. But Farouk nodded and, without taking his gaze from them, repeated his request for Hackney to release his panicking monkey. 'Tell your men to back off, or Minki here becomes monkey history.'

'Yes, anything, just don't hurt him. He bruises so easily.'

'Let us pass and you can have your precious monkey. Tell them to throw down their weapons and let us leave here.' Farouk said a few more words and the would-be attackers begrudgingly stood back a few steps to the wall.

Both men made their way slowly past the agitated rogue's lineup. Hackney all the time, holding the monkey poised to make good on his threat should any of them make a move. Slowly, they manage to put about ten feet between themselves and their would-be attackers.

'Put Minki down now and you will not be harmed.' At this point, Littleton and Hackney turn to each other and intuitively begin to run, run for all they are worth. Both Littleton and the monkey now screaming at an equal pitch. Hackney, oblivious to the noise, keeps a firm hold of his captive.

'My monkey! My monkey! Let him go, you English pig dogs!'

They come to the end of the alley, whereupon it opens up into a wider one and then veers to the left. A lone woman on her donkey dressed all in black stops and stares as they run full pelt past her, causing the animal to startle and angrily buck and bray, losing its load of hardware and goods. They then fall, clattering to the cobbles, giving the two reporters valuable moments as they are followed by Farouk's now furious gang behind them. Farouk is much slower than his men and staggers lopsidedly without the aid of his monkey to help balance, 'You dogs will die for this!'

Meanwhile, Minki, the monkey, is not feeling well. His original state of health and all this jostling and bouncing around, coupled with this high-speed unexpected pursuit, conspire to make Minki feel very ill indeed. The 'Icky Ticki' is about to kick in again. The peanutty contents of his little monkey's stomach are now at the point of no return. He grimaces and burps, giving Hackney a clue as to his next action. Hackney tosses the monkey blindly above his head and over his shoulders. Littleton, who is slightly further ahead, doesn't notice, and the two men continue at full pelt.

As if in slow motion, Minki the monkey begins his flight through the air and it really, really doesn't agree with him. Vomit erupts from the little monkey as he spins, seemingly to spray it everywhere, as if propelled by his own in-built vomit booster rocket, he flies, thrust by a stream of projectile peanut-laden fuel.

Landing head-to-head with the first thug, knocking off his turban, causing him to slip on Minki's peanut paste-laden gastric juices. He slides and falls gracefully into the second thug, who, like a domino, collides with him and ends up tumbling to the ground, as do the third and fourth. The running reporters look back at the melee just a moment before quickening their pace to carry on sprinting out of harm's way.

As Farouk finally rounds the corner of the alley, he comes upon his would-be fellow assassins, who now lay in a tangled, vomit-dampened, defeated heap. The biggest man, with the blackest bearded chin, has one very ill monkey cradled in his arms. Littleton and Hackney just carry on at break-neck speed, running through the busy streets and alleys until they are sure they are not being followed.

'Good thinking, Hackney; where did you learn to use a monkey like that?'
'As a boy, actually, I knew it would come in handy one day.'

The streets become more populated, and gradually, they begin to feel safer in the proximity of others. More by luck, than judgment, they find themselves back at the dockside. The Doria was just where they had left her, still being unloaded of her cargo and taking more onboard.

The dock was reassuringly still teeming with people. One of them stands out in the crowd. A large man is frantically scanning the horizon from beneath a very furrowed brow. While moving backwards and forwards along the gangplank of the ship. His agitation looks acute until he spies Littleton and Hackney, then a broad smile beams across his face, but it's short-lived as he registers the two men's appearance, disheveled, sweaty without hats or jackets, and showing signs of having been slightly vomited on. Many flies hang around Littleton. The big man approaches, raising his hands in the air with the most theatrical of gestures.

'Praise be to Allah, you are safe.' The owner of the voice is dressed in the traditional and very practical garb of many of the local men, a long toga-like skirt and turban headdress. Around his neck hung a small box brownie camera with a bellowed lens. He is a stark contrast to their last acquaintance, much larger but also replete with a thick black moustache and short beard - a comforting, almost infectious innocent smile beneath it.

'My friends Doctor Hackney and Littleton.' Littleton still smarts at Hackney's 'Doctor' epithet.
'Yes,' they both reply, unsure of the big man's intentions after their last encounter.
'And may we ask who you are?' Littleton stands behind Hackney.

'My name is Farouk, Farouk Akesh,' holding out a large calloused hand in greeting, the knuckles of which were slightly wet with blood from the recent cuts. By the looks of it, they are still bleeding.

'You were tricked by Bengay Wat,' he spits venomously to the ground, catching a passing dock rat squarely between the eyes, causing it to wander blindly into the path of a heavy crate that is being lowered by a hoist to the dock. Littleton grimaces as its tail twitches involuntarily as it is crushed beneath the heavy crate. Farouk wipes his mouth with his sleeve, as if the very mention of the name had created a foul taste in his mouth.

'The swine intercepted a telegram you sent. Someone supplied him with the information about your arrival. My apologies for not being here to meet you, but he contrived it that I was otherwise engaged,' he stares at his ample, bruised fists and smiles.

The new Farouk could be taken for a jolly butcher had he a stained string apron and cleaver; fortunately, he had not. He looked cool and comfortable, swathed in the long linen dress that all the local men seem to wear and reminded the two dishevelled men that they were several degrees off cool at this present moment. The swarm of buzzing flies around Littleton only seemed to emphasise that fact further.

'Your belongings are still on board. I was told you left the dockside with Bengay and then endeavoured to find you as quickly as possible. But forgive me I was unable. You have had to deal with him?'

'Oh, we had to deal with him alright, we don't take no piffle, we're English,' Littleton announces proudly.

'Then you two are a more formidable team than I had at first thought.' Farouk smiles. Like a cat on a warm windowsill, both men take this compliment well, as they receive so few. 'You were tricked by that demon Bengay-Wat and his damn monkey Minki,' Farouk says loudly. Littleton nods. Farouk adds, 'That is not his monkey's real name either, by the way; his real name is Winky, but he hates that name.'

'Minki was Winky the Monkey?' asks Littleton. 'Yes.'

'Minki was Winky, but no more... ' 'Winky and Wat,' Hackney says.

'The Monkey,' says Littleton, 'he just said so.' Hackney looks on confused.

'He said he was you,' says Hackney, looking to Farouk. 'Winky the monkey, can speak?' Littleton asks, puzzled by this revelation.

'Can he?' gasps Hackney.

'Wat, said he was you,' replied Littleton to Farouk. 'Not the monkey?' replied Farouk.

'Did he?' says Hackney, frowning. 'I never heard him say that,' adds Hackney.

'No, I meant Wat!' Littleton gasps, exasperated. 'He said he was you, not the monkey. Winky or Minki or whatever his name is didn't say anything. Wat said he was you, Farouk Akesh. Is everyone clear on that note?'

Nobody seems particularly clear, but they continue.

'It was his case of Icky Ticki that helped us escape.' 'What's Icky Tiki?' asks Farouk.

'No Minki had the Icky Ticki. Wat was just a scoundrel of the first order, but he didn't have Icki Tiki, just his monkey Minki.' 'Minki the monkey, he didn't say anything because he's a monkey, right? Everyone is clear?' Littleton continued. 'We followed him into a trap, but Hackney and I got the better of them by using the monkey and his current stomach disorder, coupled with some damn fine leg work. We were able to make our escape.' Littleton pauses to swat a fly off the end of his nose. He turns to Farouk and eyes him suspiciously.

'All clear?'

The conversation pauses...

'Wait a minute, how do we know you are the real Farouk?' The big man looks around him as if searching for an answer. 'I have no monkey!' He laughs with an infectious deep bellow.

Littleton and Hackney manage a half-hearted smile. The big man puts his hands on the shoulders of each of his charges as they go into more detail about their ordeal and make their way back to the ship.

'Your rooms are booked at the Hotel Casbah; someone knew of your arrival details, all right? Both of the telegrams sent by you and received were intercepted. I think we should have a word with the ship's wireless operator, don't you?'

They follow Farouk as he moves about the ship looking for the wireless room. After obtaining directions from one of the more helpful stewards, they enter a door marked, 'Keep Out Wireless Room.' It becomes apparent that it is not a wireless room. But erroneously signposted as such as a prank by an aggrieved signwriter who was dismissed on the last voyage. They enter another door next to that one. It's marked 'Madam FiFi's'.

'Ah, Madame FiFi?' enquires Farouk to a round and pudgy little man who lowers his spectacles as he eats a banana at his radio set.

'Harold Bride, actually. Can I help you?'

'We think you can.' All three men stand around the operator making him rather uncomfortable. Littleton does the questioning. He absent-mindedly picks up a banana from the desk, using it as one would handle a gun, pointing it squarely at Bride on assuming the role of the interrogator.

'You are the wireless operator?'

'You know I am, I just told you. Here is my wireless, this is my office.'

'Hmmm... don't get tricky, Bride.'

'Doctor Hackney, there has had me send two messages and he has received another two further ones.' Littleton is quite surprised by this.

'Is that true, Hackney?'

'You know it is. I did tell you. They are the details from Lady Fern about the trip.'

'What am I supposed to be asking then Farouk?' asks Littleton somewhat exasperatedly. Farouk takes over the questioning.

'Did anyone else see those messages, has anyone on board been in here besides yourself and been able to read private messages in detail?'

Harold shifts uneasily in his chair and adjusts his collar.

'Well, to be honest, a rather attractive young lady took a fascination in the Marconigraph and all its workings, including me,' he smiled. 'Something of a stunning young beauty she was.'
'And this beauty was by chance called Sonia Sinclair... was she?'
'Sonia Sinclair was, yes. By jove she was pretty clever too, we have become very close. I showed her how all the equipment works-'
Littleton then says with a sneer, 'I bet you did.'
'And,' Harold continues without missing a beat, 'So I suppose she may have seen some of the messages. What's all this about then?'
'So besides being able to access any of the incoming and outgoing private messages she could presumably send her own.'
'Could do and did. She was a competent operator within just a few days.'

All the men's suspicions were confirmed.

'Thank you, Harold, you have been most helpful.' The men returned to their cabin and thankfully find that the bags are still inside.

'When I had heard you left here with Wat, I didn't have your bags loaded onto my cart, I thought I might be shipping your personal effects back to England along with your remains.' The deep, hearty laugh echoed around the cabin. Littleton and Hackney smile uneasily.

'Before we check into the hotel Casbah, I think we will check out the Wondering Camel, that your friend Bengay Wat mentioned.' He spits on the floor at the utterance of his name. 'We may learn something. Tourists and foreigners never go there, or if they do, they wish they hadn't. It is filled with low life, but you are with me, you are highlife. It is on our way through the bazaar with a shortcut. I have a few questions to ask, so we will have what you English say... an evening tipple.'

Chapter Six
A Trap?

The discordant music, such as it is, ceases instantly. A distinct hush falls upon the smoke-filled room. All eyes turn to the conspicuous trio, as they push through the paint-peeled swinging doors into the dimly-lit sweaty dive that is the Wandering Camel. Farouk leads the way.

The three men make their way over to a table and sit down at a small overturned barrel and some battered wooden stools, the only empty seats in the place. It enjoys a higher vantage point of the down-market establishment beside a large potted pineapple palm. A pensive silence falls across the lips of the unruly customers, followed by hushed whispers as the rabble of scruffy clientele stares at the three new arrivals.

They are the instant focal point and unwanted centre of attention. A cross-legged pipe-playing Bedda gradually resumes his tuneless blowing, the colourful death's head cobra dances before the turbaned snake-charmer as he blows his small wooden flute. Littleton stares at the somewhat familiar snake as it withdraws into the darkness of its basket.

'I think that's the snake from the boat,' he whispers to Hackney.

Littleton checks his collar, sliding a finger between it and his moist skin as he nervously scans the hostile faces of the bar. Oil lamps and candles mounted in chipped, dark bottles serve to illuminate the thick fog that lingers in the air from the bubbling hookah pipes around them. The smell of hashish is strong and savoured by Farouk as he smiles, drawing deep into his nostrils, almost oblivious to the reaction their entrance has caused.

Almost, but not quite.

Farouk turns his head and returns the glare of a particularly unsavory character casting an unwanted interest in the trio. Farouk's brow furrows deeply as he holds the man's gaze. The war of wills goes on for a few moments; the other combatant eventually looks to the stone-tiled floor and then turns away, recognising that Farouk is maybe not to be so easily intimidated; he returns to his game on the table, but not before casting a last sneer in the men's general direction.

Slowly muted talking resumes and the atmosphere returns. A bongo and tambourine strike up, whilst a lone banjo player, strumming away, strangely forms part of the band. The musical fare serves as a beat to accompany a rather heavy belly dancer, who now continues her shimmering routine. Her filmy-bejewelled costume does its best to restrain her buxom form as it sways hypnotically to the odd beat. Her arms sway and flutter in an agitated rhythm, shaking the tiny silver castanets at the tips of each of her outstretched fingers.

Farouk gestures to a waitress, a curvy woman in a simple gauze costume with heavy, dark eye makeup and many bangles on her wrists and arms. She approaches, somewhat reluctantly, as Littleton and Hackney try and look as tough as it was possible for two very out-of-place, nervous English men. It was obvious that they were completely beyond their depth in the present environment but, stoically, they made every effort to appear unintimidated. Even returning some of the glances cast in their direction to the utter infuriation of the rabble situated around them.

A nasty-looking little fellow sits a few short yards from Littleton, playing with a large knife. He stabs its blade furiously between the spread fingers of his outstretched hand flattened on the table. Judging from his bloody, bleeding fingers, he is not good at this game.

He is missing his right ear and sports an old, shiny scar that runs across the length of his beard-stubbled face. He stops the knife play and stares motionless at Littleton. His stature is very short and he looks to carry the features of dwarfism. His female partner (equally unappealing) displays all the signs of having consumed too much intoxicant and joins him in the glaring competition. The pair grin at Littleton, looking at nothing other than Littleton. The woman who gives only a very slight indication of belonging to the female species, inserts her cocked little finger up one of her gaping nostrils. Furiously, she rummages up its farthest recesses until, smiling, she finds what she is looking for.

The offending nasal blockage is retrieved, and she sits atop her little finger. Littleton is mortified by the actions of this harpy as he watches her roll her find between her thumb and forefinger. Despite the nauseous display, he is unable to avert his gaze as he begins to feel queasy. He finally turns away quickly, just as with a bony flick of a finger, she sends the projectile zipping inches past his nose. He follows its track and watches it splash into someone's drink to his right.

The waitress arrives.

'Are you lost?'

Farouk smiles and shakes his head, 'Only in my admiration for you, my pretty lady.'
'I'm Monique. We don't get many tourists in The Camel. What'll it be?'
'We are not lost, but maybe you can help me?' The big man smiles at the woman.

She is attractive and unlike most of the women they have met since they arrived, she is not swathed head to foot in black cloth. Far from it, her costume leaves little to the imagination. The two Englishmen are momentarily distracted by her raw beauty and, for a moment, can forget about the uneasy situation they now find themselves in and concentrate on the more appealing vision before them. The waitress seems to view all with equal contempt.

'Well, what are you drinking?' she snaps.

'Three large Yaca,' Farouk holds up three fingers to Monique.

'Tell me, Monique, do you know of a small man, a cripple, with a monkey. I've heard he comes here often.'
'He owns this place, what do you want with him?'
'Oh, I have information that he would find most useful.'

The waitress begins to laugh and tosses her mane of ebony hair as she retreats with her tray to a doorway off the bar. The three men say nothing. Someone belches loudly in the distance and, by way of accompaniment, the dwarf's female partner breaks wind with a staccato response almost simultaneously. It's a real crowd pleaser and everyone laughs heartily in the immediate vicinity.

The decoration of the Camel has been kept to a minimum. The walls are devoid of anything, save the spider web-like patterns of cracking, damp plaster. A single, large wooden-bladed fan turns slowly on the ceiling. Gripping one of the wooden blades as it sweeps around is a large hairy spider, Littleton eyes it uneasily in recognition. It looks very much like a tarantula. The waitress returns with the drinks, slamming them belligerently down on the table.

'I hope they choke you,' she walks away muttering something to herself.
'So how do you like the Camel?' asks Farouk. 'What camel?' says Littleton.
'He means here, that's what this place is called,' Hackney reminds him.
'It's not exactly the Dog and Duck, is it?'
Farouk lowers his voice to a whisper, 'Do you see anyone you recognise amongst this lowlife? Anyone from the alleyway who attacked you?'

The two men stare around without trying to attract anyone's attention not making eye contact with anyone. 'I don't recognise anyone do you, Hackney?' Littleton speaks quickly. It is obvious he doesn't want any trouble.

Unfortunately, Hackney has not thought that far ahead from his gaze and his concentrated, fixed frown. Littleton's heart sinks as he sees that spark of recognition in his friend's eyes. Casting his eyes back to the rotating spider waiting inevitably for his fears to be realised.

'I think I do,' Hackney frowns in the direction of the swinging doors through which they had entered.
'Oh hell,' Littleton whispers under his breath. The two men follow Hackney's gaze to see a large, rough-looking character whom Littleton, too, recognises as one of Bengay's thugs. The character who had spoken to Bengay after Hackney had grabbed his monkey. He was standing at the doors, he looks towards the three men, and quickly scans the room before making his way across the crowded bar and then entering a swinging door marked private.

Littleton and Hackney watch from behind the palm leaves. The waitress, who had served them, approaches the door at the bar and knocks before entering after him.

'The sparks may fly now,' Farouk smiles as he outstretches his arms and cracks his knuckles one by one. Then, taking his glass of Yaka, he downs it in one gulp. Hackney, in turn, follows suit and does the same. Giving only a slight indication that the brew was indeed as strong as the colonic contents of a camel's lower intestine. Littleton lifts his glass of clear liquid, sniffing it suspiciously before likewise doing the same.

Unfortunately, Littleton's disposition, and more fragile constitution not being as strong as his comrades, deals with the consumed libation in a whole different manner as his body begins to shake. The Yaka, from Littleton's mouth, shoots across the table in a powerful hose-like jet, his accompanying scream could be discerned as trying to get away from his constricting throat that he was now clutching. The Yaka, like a fluid javelin headed, reached, impaled, and then dissolved in an all-enveloping splash of showering droplets on the dwarf who had been giving Littleton such a hard time earlier.

The dwarf sits motionless for a moment, then starts to wobble imperceptibly at first then with more discernible movement. His eyes blaze ferociously as he faces Hackney who points quickly to Littleton. The angry dwarf gets down from his chair giving all the signs of being about to explode, twitching and shrugging his shoulders almost in an involuntary manner.

Littleton tries to take some relief, that once down from his chair, he is even shorter than he had first appeared. The relief is short-lived as he unsheathes the huge, shiny knife that he had been caressing earlier.

At the same moment, the swinging doors are flung open by the two long hairy arms of Minki or Winky the monkey. Sitting atop the shoulders of Bengay Wat who wobbles awkwardly into the bar and surveys the surroundings. He stands, swaying and now blocking their escape. Both he and his monkey are smiling, he folds his arms. The monkey keeps his balance by using an outstretched arm on the nearby stone pillar.

Again, the attention in the bar is focused on the trio as an uneasy silence is broken. The door to the office marked private opens. A new face appears as unsavoury as the rest of the surrounding crew, accompanied by one more of the thugs they messed up earlier in the alleyway. The sound of chairs scraping across the floor and people taking positions around them does not give any cause for comfort; Farouk sits looking almost bored by the developments. The two Englishmen apprehensively wait for the inevitable attack to proceed. Desperately maintaining their position whilst praying for salvation. Both keep that firm stiff British upper lip, as all Englishmen do in such situations. For God, King and country.

The moment is broken by Farouk, seeming to snap out of his nonchalance, picks up his chair with great speed and agility (for a big man) and smashes it down on the table, breaking it into many pieces - but retaining the heavy, wooden legs in each hand. He smiles menacingly with a confident grin, then swiftly takes a threatening stance against anyone daring to approach. Hackney picks up one of the smaller discarded legs. Littleton, wide-eyed, fumbles for a weapon, he reaches into his pockets and pulls out one of Harold Brides' lunch items that he had inadvertently taken from the radio operator. He whips it out, pointing it like a gun. He menacingly holds it, aiming like you would a loaded pistol, well, as menacingly as you can hold a browning banana.

The attack comes.

They are rushed from all sides. The dwarf steps forward, snarling and slashing. He receives a forceful blow from Hackney across the side of the head, unsteadying him and causing a bloody piece of skin to protrude above his right eye.

The banshee-like wail of his ugly female partner pierces the room as she grapples with Littleton on the floor after diving from the table. Littleton, in turn, is screaming equally as loud.

131

Farouk has two men on each arm. A spin of his body loosens their grip on him. He smiles and punches a turbaned would-be assailant between the eyes, smashing the chair leg into his face for good measure.

The belly dancer and the band also pitch in; it seems the odds are insurmountable. The harpy that Littleton is now grappling with more furiously, has his hair in her clenched fist, both screaming with equal measure.

Fists fly, and the sound of broken wood, glass, and bones fills the air. The banjo player, for some unaccountable reason, starts playing a raucous bluegrass accompaniment to the mayhem.

Minki, the monkey, hops from Bengay's shoulders and enters the melee, jumping for the ceiling fan, screaming, and hanging on for several rotations, counting the revolutions before dropping into the fracas.

Against all the odds, it begins to look as if the trio are gaining ground. They fight for all they are worth. Farouk seems to be in charge of every encounter; most attacks are swatted off like flies. As he goads two unsure combatants into an attack, he makes the mistake of turning his back on a wooden side booth that had looked to be empty - it was not.

From behind the booth, the belly dancer appears standing quickly on the seat. She holds above her head a heavy cast glass distilling vessel. She brings this crashing down on Farouk's head, with all the force she can muster. For a moment, it looks as if he can weather the blow, but his eyes glaze; he stops his attack and drops his arms to receive two more heavy blows in quick succession from the man in front of him. Smiling, his knees hit the floor and his unconscious bulk topples forward.

He is out for the count.

With the main firepower down, the crowd concentrates on the two Englishmen still standing. Despite a valiant effort without Farouk, they are massively outnumbered and overcome.

It is over.

****

Consciousness is reached along a dark tunnel. Hackney wakes first to the sound of Littleton's ticking nose and the sight of his two friends bruised and bound. They are all tied to posts that look to be wooden supports that reach from the floor to the ceiling.

Their prison is a damp cellar, presumably of the Wandering Camel. Slowly, as his focus returns, he becomes aware that the three of them are not alone. A large, ugly brute stands in front of them, smiling sadistically at his three captive charges. Blocking any escape (should they magically be able to remove their bonds) and make for the door. A small, barred window gives the impression that the room is purpose-built for such a use as the men find themselves in at present. As the two others come around, it is Littleton who speaks first, possibly without thinking.

'I say you, I say, you filthy brute, what have you done to us and why are we tied up?'

The dark and filthy, but powerfully built brute of a gentleman, to whom Littleton has addressed, frowns hard at his most vocal outburst.

Hackney looks worried, 'I say, steady-on Littleton I think you may have taken a knock to the head,'
Littleton ignores his friend's advice.
'Leave this to me; I'm a pretty skilled negotiator; it's all about projection, not what you say but how you say it,' he whispers to Hackney and Farouk.
'You, big fellow, we are English, we will take no chit-chat from no nit-wits do you savey - hokey cokey, do you comprehend?'
The big fellow moves quickly across the floor to within inches of Littleton. Littleton turns to the two other men, 'I think I'm getting through.'

The big fellow moves uncomfortably closer. His breath is warm and vile upon Littleton's now wide-eyed features. Now, quite alert features at this point. The ugly brute noisily conjures up a mouthful of phlegm and dispatches it hard into Littleton's face. The guard smiles and resumes his position, arms folded, standing in front of the heavily bolted door, leaving Littleton to stare at the string of shiny gelatinous phlegm slowly dripping from his nose.

He begins to silently sob.

A moment passes and the steel lock is tripped and the heavy bolt withdrawn. The guard chuckles as he leaves the room.

'This is turning into quite a day, are the evenings as much fun?' asks Hackney half-heartedly.
'It is good you retain your sense of humour, English. I have a feeling we will all need one.'

There is a slight pause in the conversation as a large black rat scurries across the cold stones of the cellar floor and catches a small mouse by the neck, shaking it vigorously before disappearing with his meal into an open crevice in the wall.

Farouk indicates silently that he needs the men's attention by nodding his head and mouthing the words 'listen'.

He speaks very quietly so as to not alert the guard. 'Listen to me, I'm not who you think I am.'

'You're another imposter?'

'No. I am a duly deputised officer of the law. Sergeant Farouk Akesh at your service. I have been assigned to you as part of our investigation. We have someone working undercover here. This is where most of the goods are crated and boxed before shipping. Look at the marks on those crates to your right.'

The two men peer in the direction Farouk has indicated. Several stacked crates have a small black scarab beetle stamped across them.

'The Egyptian SUTI has been working for months to trap these counterfeiters and smugglers who are robbing our country blind. We are to meet an English agent at the hotel should we be able to get out of this alive. He is to accompany us on the expedition dig,' he pauses '… It may have been a mistake coming here.'

'Might have been … you think?' Littleton moans, his face glistening with the guard's saliva.

The echo of heavy footsteps is heard as people approach the cellar door.

'Be silent,' Farouk whispers quickly. A turbaned man in khaki shorts and some sort of decorated military outfit enters the room along with Bengay and Minki his monkey. Who, despite having a black eye, looks over the three captives gleefully.

'These are the ones?' The uniform asks Bengay as the two men stare at the three captives. Farouk, Littleton, and Hackney stare back in silence.

'Yes, they have injured many customers and caused much damage, it is terrible,' smiles Bengay.
'What! We were attacked, and he's tied us up,' shouts Littleton, nodding his unrestrained head frantically in Bengay's direction. Bengay wobbles towards Littleton.

'It is Mr. Wat to you, and there are over fifty witnesses upstairs who would say otherwise.'
Littleton, unperturbed, continues, 'You are the one who attacked us. Twice in one day, you are the one who has tied us up! You scoundrel!'

'And so shall you remain if you keep making these false accusations.' The turbaned man speaks with an air of authority and the captives notice for the first time his shiny badge.

'I am Sergeant Koresh. I am the Law & Order here; you men cannot cause trouble in this fine establishment. This is not one of your English pubs. This is not your Dog and Duck. Your weapons have been confiscated and will remain as evidence against you.'
'What weapons?' asks Hackney. Farouk speaks, 'It is futile to argue.'
'Very wise, big man, your friends would do well to learn from you.'

Two more men enter the room; they are Bengay's men. He speaks to them, but Littleton and Hackney understand nothing of it. The policeman continues, his arms behind his back.

'As it happens, you are very lucky men. Mr. Wat here is feeling very kind and forgiving today. You should be grateful to him that he is not going to press charges where a thousand would. This is not England and you would do well to remember that. You cannot just get off the boat here and come and cause trouble, do you understand?'

Littleton is about to protest more as Koresh takes out his truncheon.

'Do you understand?'

The waitress that had served them enters the cellar; they are becoming something of a spectacle. Now more modestly dressed at present and carrying a small satchel. She has finished her shift. Walking up to Hackney and pressing herself close to him, she begins teasing and stroking his bruised face. The two thugs with Bengay and the policeman laugh. They sneer, mildly amused by this.

Speaking a few words to each other in Arabic, Monique runs her fingers over the restrained Hackney. Hackney remains wide-eyed and stoic, staring straight ahead, trying to ignore the treacherous beauty as she runs her hands over his bruised face and tousled hair. He doesn't move but thinks solely of England as he feels her passing her probing hands dancing over his clothing. After a few moments, she tires of her game, and with a sneer, she gives up.

'Ha, these foreign fools are such dead fish,' she moves away in disgust.

The Turbaned police officer speaks again, 'If I come across you again, then maybe no one will come across you again ever. Do we understand each other? Now, a thank you to Mr Wat from you,' says Koresh, staring at Littleton. 'What?' gasps Littleton. 'That's Mr Wat to you,' smiles Bengay enjoying himself immensely. 'Now apologise to Mr Wat on your way out, he is a very kind man,' adds Koresh.

The three thugs and Monique, the waitress, stand with Koresh and Bengay as they are released and unbound. The detainees are now free. They troop defeatedly past the lineup, Littleton being the last one out past their captors.

In a final act of vindictive humiliation, the monkey cups his hand, licks it, spits into his palm and smacks Littleton hard on the back of the head as they shuffle out of the cellar. Without thinking, Littleton spins around and lunges at the little ape, grabbing it around the throat.

Almost as quickly, the thugs pry him off and look to Bengay for instructions as the monkey screams blue murder. Littleton struggles hard, but is no match for the burly villains. Bengay and Koresh laugh out loud. Littleton is roughly and unceremoniously thrown into the alley after his friends.

Farouk is more ushered, than thrown, as his size commands a little more respect and less heavy-handedness. Littleton and Hackney get up from the dusty street and brush themselves off. Farouk looks back at the slammed heavy door of the

Wandering Camel, as the heavy bolt is heard loudly secured behind it.

Outside, people are finishing their business for the day as the evening sun begins to lower in the sky, casting a tangerine glow on the canvas awnings and walls. Camel and cow pats and various detritus from the market stalls are left as the local traders trundle home for the night after a day of hawking their wares. Farouk looks back one more time, at the now-closed heavy wooden door of the Wandering Camel and shakes his head. Littleton stands his left foot firmly planted in a very fresh mound of camel dung.

'I think we may have been rather foolish and a trifle impetuous in our haste to visit that den of thieves. I will plan more thoroughly next time,' Farouk frowns.

Hackney chirps up with an unexpected enthusiasm. 'That may be so, but I believe we do have one ally in there.'
'Oh,' says Littleton.
'Monique the waitress,' Hackney smiles.
'Monique, the waitress? Are you mad? What are you talking about?'
'She stuffed this down my pants,' he replies with something of a smirk.

Littleton and Farouk stand in surprise at the small snub-nosed Ely number seven repeating revolver that Hackney now holds up for them to see.

'So, it's Monique who's our agent in the Camel,' Farouk ponders the notion.
'You mean you didn't know?' Littleton asks in disbelief. 'No one tells me anything.'

Littleton sighs aloud, too tired to argue. They begin their walk back to the hotel. 'I'd have found out eventually, I always do,' Farouk adds.
'Where is the hotel Casbah?' Hackney asks, the day beginning to take its toll.
'It is barely a camel's whisker from here. In just a few moments from now, we will be washing the stench of the last few hours from our skin. We can make it before dark,' Farouk sets off ahead and the two men follow.

The air becomes cooler as they make their way through the dimly lit, constricted, narrow streets. The shutters and vented doors remain closed. Faces and shadows can be seen behind the curtains of glassless windows. Their long shadows play as dancing silhouettes in a wordless play on the pale brick and stucco walls. The three shadowy figures dissolve into the streets.

Back at the Camel, Koresh turns to Bengay the smile no longer on his face. 'Someone is getting careless, why was I called? You could have dispatched them yourself. There was no need to involve me.'

Bengay shakes his head. 'Too many witnesses. We have a party of fish salters in on a weekend special. Not all the people in the bar tonight are aware of our activities in the export business.'

He shifts unsteadily on his feet. His monkey, Minki leans its outstretched arms against the beam.

'We have possession of the next consignments and replicas. The presence of foreigners was something I was not prepared for until this morning. They were unexpectedly lucky enough to escape my first attempt at silencing them, which is just as well. Because the big fellow who is with them now is also with the SUTI.'
'What?' Koresh is mildly shocked, then annoyed by this revelation.
'His identification was found when we searched them. The two foreigners are involved in something. I can't work out what at the moment, but we need to know how many more are involved and whether they need to be diverted or removed. I wanted to talk to you before I acted too hastily.'

'It was by chance they escaped?' Koresh asks, his agitation showing.

'Of course. A chance in a thousand. They are stupid, but they are also lucky.'

'Perhaps their luck is about to run out? Deal with them tonight, if possible, or first thing tomorrow. Their expedition to our beloved mother Egypt ends here.'

'It is done.' Bengay smiles...

The two men laugh an evil cackle. 'Ha-hahaha-hahaha -aaa - ha... Ha... '

'Shut up,' Koresh closes down the moment of camaraderie.

In the shadows behind some crates, they don't see the dark, sultry features of Monique, the waitress, listening intently. Her bosom is hot and heaving as she listens to the plot they are sinisterly weaving.

Chapter Seven
The Hotel Casbah

Three hours later, the three men stand in the lobby of the Hotel Casbah beneath the flashing neon sign proclaiming, Hotel Casbah. A contributing factor to the time spent trying to find the hotel was the fact that the sign for the hotel was inside the marbled floored lobby, making it impossible to view it from the street outside.

The desk clerk informed them that the hotel sign was an expensive later addition, and was much safer inside rather than out. As outside it could and would be stolen, as had the thirteen signs before it. The previous thirteen hotel signs had been much sought after because there were many Hotel Casbahs in the area.

Five in this very street - all decked with signs looking very similar to the previously purloined signs. The Hotel Casbah being a very popular name for a hotel in these parts, making the signs something of a highly desirable commodity.

While the clerk checks that their rooms are ready, the men take repose in large comfortable, upholstered, velvet-tasselled seats around the stone lobby fountain. The comings and goings of the hotel hold their attention as Farouk clears his throat.

'Gentlemen, I have not told you the full extent of my involvement with you. I am your guide, but I am also a part-time officer in the Egyptian SUTI,' he says the word SUTI with something of a flourish.
'You already told us.' 'I did?'
Both men nod in the affirmative.

'The SUTI?' both men ask. 'What does it stand for?'
'The Special Undercover Treasure Investigation ... Squad.' 'That would be SUTI's,' Littleton corrects him.
'We don't use the last 's' as it is silent and it makes it sound well - a little silly.'
'Yes, it would,' Littleton agrees.
'I am on assignment to gather as much information as possible about the infamous Black Scarab smuggling ring.'

The hotel sign blinked on and off in the distance as two dark figures removed it.

'For months now, the SUTI has been tracking the haemorrhaging flow of valuable Egyptian artefacts from this country. Both public and private collections seem to lose innumerable pieces that somehow find their way into Bengay's sticky fingers, and then onto the Black Scarab's many-tentacled grasp. All the pieces are either unlicensed or stolen, and then illegally exported. It is difficult to obtain a license for contraband. Many of our rare and valuable mummies are stolen and destroyed once on the continent. We are losing mummies like there is no tomorrow, and they are not making any more, as you know. I can tell you it is a situation that we can't tolerate any longer. Sergeant Koresh has been bought and paid for. He turns a blind eye and provides protection for a percentage - should anyone dig too deep.'

The two Englishmen listen intently.

'We know they are operating out of the Wandering Camel. We are here to dig deep, very deep.'
'So, what's our part in all this? The Chantress, does she exist?' asks Littleton.
'We have a map that suggests she does. It was drawn by Professor Saunders. Have you heard of him? Like yourselves he was an Englishman too?'

Littleton and Hackney exchange glances at the mention of Saunders and a map.

'We have heard the tale, we read about it in the papers, he's still missing, isn't he?' asks Hackney.
'Not missing, though unfortunately, he was found quite mad wandering in the desert. It is this map that gave Lord Fern the idea for his expedition.' Farouk gestures with a smile.
'It may match the one Elizabeth gave us. A madman's map, it's a bit of a longshot, isn't it?' Hackney says.

Littleton quizzes Farouk, 'A piece of stone bearing strange writing you say?' Both men are intrigued as Farouk continues.

'Ingredients and quantities written in ancient symbols. Yes, Saunders was not initially insane. Have you heard of Saunders Crackers makers of savory snacks and dry wheat confections?'
'What? I'll say they are the best damn salty crackers you can get!' Hackney smiles.
'Well, Professor Saunders used the information on the stone to create what he believed to be the very crackers used at the sacrificial ceremonies in which the Chantress took part. He set up a hugely successful business and returned to Egypt to see what other aperitifs might be hidden amongst the ancient sands. He would market the crackers as authentic, Ancient Egyptian snacks of the highest order that were popular not only in England but with the locals here, in fact, worldwide.'

'Brilliant!' both the Englishmen exclaim.

Farouk's eyes flick around the lobby...

'Yes brilliant, and yet stupid. The crackers were cursed, you see, there was also an issue with the quantities.'
'What do you mean quantities?'
'The amount of ingredients used in the crackers,' frowns Farouk.
'Oh, I see. But what about the curse... ?'
'He was not so lucky the second time, on his subsequent quest. After a disagreement over unpaid wages, he was left entombed in an empty walled chamber, a royal latrine by a dishonest and ruthless villain whom you have met... Bengay Wat.' Again, Farouk spits on the floor at the mention of Wat's name. 'For many years, he was lost, so his daughter administered the business of running the company, which she does very well. The proceeds of which go towards the running of many charitable concerns, so I hear.'

Farouk takes a breath and continues.

'One of which is the Sanatorium Lunatique, ironically, its most important benefactor is also a patient who is now incarcerated within its very walls. He's quite mad and he and his cracker Empire pay for the upkeep. Saunder's mind has gone, but not completely; sometimes, he is lucid. But he is, for the most part, as you say, crackers, and it is his cracker empire that keeps him there. He and his daughter have lived there on-site for the last few years. Lord Fern and Saunders go way back; he had known Saunders for many years before Egypt; back in England, I think they were at Eton together reading history. They both believed in the Chantress as I do. We are to meet with Saunders and his daughter tomorrow. We will be able to ask her any questions that might help us. I am told she doesn't miss much that goes on in this town, but she's something of a mystery; an elusive character herself, although I have never met her.'

The hotel clerk approaches.

'Your rooms are ready, sirs; the luggage arrived this afternoon. Have a pleasant stay in Egypt at the Hotel Casbah.' Handing the two sets of keys to them the clerk smiles, then suddenly remembers something else.

'Oh, sir, there were three gentlemen here earlier looking for you.'
'Really,' frowns Farouk.
'I said you hadn't arrived yet and they seemed very disappointed.' All three men stare nervously around the lobby at the clerk's news.
'They were most helpful carrying your bags up to your room for you, though.'
'You let them take our bags?'

'They were most insistent.' Farouk is not pleased with this news. 'After they left, this arrived also for you.' The clerk hands a large manilla envelope marked, 'Top Secret' in bright red letters to Farouk adding, 'Do you think you might get my pen back from his monkey if at all possible?'
'His monkey?'
'Yes, very odd fellow, seemed to have trouble keeping his balance; it's very strange that he said he would return tomorrow as it was very important.'

The clerk smiles, unaware of the consternation his news brings to the three men.

'Hmm…we better get some sleep we may need our wits about us tomorrow. I feel as if we have been up for days. Whatever Bengay wants it will keep until tomorrow. I'll go through the brief contained in the envelope and catch up on the operation notes in my room. We will meet at 6 am.'

The hotel looks to be closing for the night and all three look well-worn with the tumultuous day of events prepare to turn in for the night.

'Goodnight, gentlemen. Sleep well; you have had an interesting but, I'm sure, weary day.'
'Good night, Farouk.'

'Do you suppose they serve the surgery breakfast cereal in the different colours?'
'I have no idea.'
'I like those,' Hackney muses. 'Maybe I will read these briefing notes in the morning when I am fresh,' yawns Farouk.
'Good idea,' both Littleton and Hackney agree. 'Everything is better after a good night's sleep.'
'Sleep tight, don't let the bed bugs bite.'

****

The unlikely team meet for breakfast. The lobby is already busy with porters, baggage clerks and guests going about their business. Luggage and bags sit around on trolleys, the large paddled ceiling fans spinning slowly above them, a welcome addition.
'Did you sleep well?' asks Farouk. 'Terrible, you?'
'I slept the sleep of a thousand camels.' 'Is that good?'
'It is not.'

They are ushered to a white table-clothed breakfast setting.

'I say, Farouk, those scoundrels have taken the map that Ms Fern gave us. They must have gone through our bags.'

Hackney conveys this news as they sit down. 'May they be visited by a thousand Tsetse flies, the Gods are working against us, this is a setback.'

A modestly dressed woman approaches and serves the sliced grapefruit with a smile. The serving staff, bright white China plates and tulip vases are a stark contrast of civility after last night's visit to the retail establishment known as the Wandering Camel. Farouk opens the manila envelope the clerk gave him last night. As he reads the contents, his eyes widen and then narrow to a frown. With a small cough, he clears his throat.

'Hmm, we also seem to have a few things not quite going to plan according to the instructions here.'
'Oh, like what?'
'Well, it says here quite clearly, under no circumstances lose the English woman Sinclair. Follow her at all costs. Do not make yourself known to Bengay Wat, as it would be dangerous to do so. Steer clear of the Wandering Camel. Avoid any contact with Sergeant Koresh; we believe him to be heavily involved; he must not learn of your true identity and do not stay at the Hotel Casbah tonight. Your location has been compromised - it could be a dangerous trap.'
'Okay, we can get the last thing right by checking out of here as soon as possible!'
'These instructions should have been read last night.'

Farouk berates himself.

'So, what does that mean? - We have stayed here and nothing
has happened - we are unharmed and quite well this morning?'
Hackney speaks for all of them.
'But for how long?' Littleton asks.
'And I didn't find that breakfast cereal I was rather hoping for,'
Hackney adds.
There is a small folded piece of paper next to Hackney's
grapefruit slice that at first, he hadn't noticed.

'I say, what's this?' Picking it up and unfolding it. He reads the
handwritten words slowly aloud...

*'You are in great danger. Take the disguises you will
find under your beds. Make your way quickly to the
Sanatorium Lunatique. Seek out cell 221B.*
Trust me.
P.S. Do not eat the grapefruit.

Signed M.S.'

Littleton spits the grapefruit slice from his mouth. The chunk of
half-chewed fruit flies across the table and bounces on the tiled
floor. His eyes wandered quickly around the room.

154

'What do you make of it? Who is this mysterious M.S. and trust him for what? What's wrong with the grapefruit? And what did he mean by disguises? What disguises?' Littleton scans the room once more.

'Well, I, for one, would like to find out.' Farouk stands, throwing his napkin down. The three men, casually, as they are able to, leave the breakfast table and head out of the room, travelling across the marble-floored foyer as nonchalantly as possible. Trying not to arouse anyone's attention, they move around the fountain and up the stairs. A bit of a commotion is heard behind them as an unfortunate waiter slips on Littleton's coughed-up fruit segment, sending him and his fully laden tray to the smooth marble-tiled floor.

From the shadows, two burly, dark characters use the commotion for cover, as likewise they do the same and follow the three men up the stairs, almost unseen.

Once inside the room, Hackney pulls a wrapped package from under the bed. Farouk and Littleton wait in anticipation as he unwraps it.
'Why don't we just get packed and get out of here?' 'Do you still have the revolver the waitress gave you?' 'It is in the top drawer of the dresser,' nods Hackney
quizzically, holding up what looks to be some random native woman's clothing.

Littleton retrieves the shiny black sidearm, he holds it reassuringly and menacingly.

'Not many people will argue with a taste of lead,' he smiles.

Littleton takes the gun, breaks the barrel, and checks the chamber to see if it is loaded, groaning at the disappointing discovery that it is not.

'Hmm, no bullets,' he flips the barrel back into place, hefting the gun in his hands. Extending his arm and raising the empty pistol theatrically at a spot on the bedroom door. Square-jawed and squinty-eyed, doing his best impression of a New York gangster.

'Take this, you filthy swine, eat lead!'

He levels the gun and gently pulls the trigger. The unloaded gun goes off with a loud, thunderous flash. Scaring the absolute stuffing out of all of them. And causing Littleton to scream and throw down the weapon like a hot potato.

Almost to the accompaniment of the bang of the pistol shot and Littleton's piercing scream, was another scream. It came from the other side of the door. Then a dull thud, like someone hitting the corridor floor after being shot.

Then a gurgle. Two gurgles. Then a cough and another scream... then another thud.

All three men stare at the bullet hole in the door. No one speaks. Hackney breaks the silence.
'I thought you said it had no bullets,' he walks over to the door and examines the small round hole with his finger.
'Did you hear the sound on the other side of the door?'
'Yes, I heard it too,' Farouk adds.
'What do you suppose that was?' asks Littleton feebly, with a hint of a tremble in his voice.

The other two men approach the door, Littleton reaches for the handle, then turns to Hackney, 'Remember what Koresh said about any more trouble?'

Hackney nods as Littleton grips the handle and slowly pulls the now bullet-pierced door towards him. All three were fully expecting to find the recipient of Littleton's unloaded gun lying on the floor outside.

There is nothing. The corridor is empty, save for a small, dark blood smear at the bottom of the door frame extending onto the polished marble floor tiles.

They all take a step forward to peek over the handrail at the foyer floor below. The gathered crowd are all staring at the limp, lifeless body now sprawled in the middle of the lobby floor. The widening pool of dark blood spreading slowly from beneath his head.

A man that they recognised from the alley, a man who now no longer felt the pain from the gunshot wound to his chest. A dead man who would no longer feel anything again... at all.

'Let's get out of here,' Littleton says, turning towards the others.

A few moments later, three very awkward and large women leave the room; aware of some commotion; they join the crowd of other inquisitive guests, staring over the balcony that runs in front of the rooms, looking down onto the central foyer and fountain. The three men are now disguised as local Arab washerwomen.

The small crowd buzzes around the body and flinches as they survey the victim of the 'fall.' The three men stare wide-eyed and are stunned at the scenario below. They do all indeed recognise the dead man as one of Bengay Wat's thugs, one they had first met in the alley and then subsequently at the Wandering Camel.

'We're for it now,' exclaims Hackney.
'I didn't mean to do that; I thought it was empty. We're going to be arrested and thrown into prison. Do you know what happens to men like us in prison?' says Littleton, now contemplating his fate dressed as a woman.

Hackney places his hands on his hips, 'What do you mean we? You shot him.'
'We need to make ourselves scarce. No one will recognise us dressed like this, we must slip away in the commotion,' Farouk takes charge.

The three large and awkward Arab women slip through the crowd, carrying their bags-and blend unnoticed into the bustle of another market day as police sirens and bells can be heard outside the hotel.

With the screech of tyres, Sergeant Koresh jumps from the car and strides furiously into the foyer with several men behind him, all rushing up the steps towards the now vacated room from which Littleton had unwittingly dispatched the loaded firearm. Koresh seethes with disappointment at his timing. Bengay, with his monkey Minki, arms outstretched, leaning on the door frame, stands behind him. 'You have let me down yet again, Mr Wat.'

Chapter Eight
Escape

No one was looking for three, large, awkward women currently making their way through the busy peopled streets and alleys past the bustling shop market fronts. Not a soul batted an eyelid as they hastily made their getaway from the hotel. The police would be looking for two white conspicuous male foreigners and a large local. Dressed as they were in the all-concealing dark linens, they were able to pass unmolested through the crowds. They would make their way toward the sanatorium. Hackney lifts his yashmak a few inches.

'Whoever M.S. is, I'm very grateful for these disguises, a stroke of genius,' Hackney mumbles.
I feel stupid, but at least we are alive,' Littleton replies. Farouk adds scratching himself in a very unladylike way that brings to the attention of Littleton that their current disguises may only work for so long.

'Look, watch and walk like me,' Littleton then does a most convincing impression of his idea of a woman walking hand on hip.

'Pssst, Professor Saunders...... Pssst.'

The professor turns from the window and faces them. Speaking confidently, he addresses the small group of odd-looking women who had called to him from the door, between the heavy, small barred window. He stands and approaches the locked door.

'Saunders... Saunders, now don't tell me, I'll get it soon, give me a moment, I know that name. I can't place the face, but I know the name. Yes, that's it! I got it I know who that is. It's me, isn't it? I'm the Professor, that's it. At your service, how may I be of assistance?'
'We have come to talk about the map, the one you had with you when you were found in the desert. The map.'
'Do you remember it?' Littleton persists.
'Of course, I do; give me a moment; I'll let you in,' Saunders smiles.
'You mean you have a key?'
'Yes, why wouldn't I? Of course, I do; I'm not crackers, you know,' he smiles as he produces a brass key, unlocks the heavy mechanism, and withdraws the solid bolt from inside,
'Although that's not true - I'm Saunders Crackers - or I was.'

Cautiously, the three men scan the empty corridor and then enter.

Welcoming them into his cell, he jovially asks, 'Well, what can I do for you, ladies?'

The professor looks very sane for someone in his position, holding out his hand and shaking all three of theirs firmly, with a vigorous handshake.

'Professor, we need to talk to you about the map.' 'The map you made,' again quizzes Hackney. 'What map?'
'You just said you remembered it,' frowns Littleton. 'Yes, before you unbolted the door?'

The three men step back and look at the now firmly bolted door behind them.

'I'm not mad, you know.' The professor smiles.
'We don't believe that you are,' Hackney speaks confidently.

Farouk is not so sure and is distracted, scratching himself vigorously - the rough fabric of the disguise beginning to irritate him.
'Then why am I here?' asked the professor. 'To get better,' Littleton smiles encouragingly.
'One day I'll leave here,' he turns to face the window.

'You're not locked in; why don't you just walk out?' asks Hackney, confused.

'Because I have to get better,' he replies. 'Better at what?'

'Being well,' he beamed. 'I was compelled to eat beetles, you know, every day, beetles for breakfast, beetles for dinner, and you know what was for supper?'

'Beetles?' all three men say in unison.

'Yes, it affected me, I'm not saying it hasn't. It was the hours, the long interminable hours. Do you know what I do to keep myself busy these days?'

All three men shake their heads silently.

'I build models. I've constructed many over the years during my incarceration.'

'Models of what?' The three of them look around the room.

'No, not models of Wat,' he spits to the floor at the mention of the scoundrel's name.

All stand back a pace from the professor.

'My models are of anything and everything, I'm working on that one at the moment. I'll show you,' he reaches up to the barred windows and takes hold of a small article, then holding it up to the light; displays it to the men.

It looks like... a beetle.

'It looks like a beetle,' Littleton spoke for everyone. 'It's a model.'

'A model, what's it made of?' Hackney draws closer.

'It's quite realistic, wouldn't you say, and you know why? Because it's made of beetle parts!'

The three men stare back at the now bolted door. They all exchange glances.

'That's what makes my models so realistic. I make them from the original parts of the original item, so they are all to scale too.'

On closer inspection, it can be discerned that the beetle has been assembled from other dead beetle parts and copious quantities of glue to form another, sort of a tiny, generic Frankenstein insect.

'I'm building a pineapple at present. Do you know what I'm using?'

'Yes, we can guess, old pineapple pieces.'

'It's not that easy; you can't get the parts in here; I've had to substitute some banana parts but not the skins, never the skins.'

The three men look around the room, now noticing that everything does seem to be a certain oddness about the assortment of objects and possessions on display. Littleton sums up everyone's thoughts. 'You are crackers.'

'Yes, gentlemen, Saunders Crackers, hardly the enterprise of a madman, wouldn't you say.'

The moment is interrupted as the lock unbolts from the outside, and the door opens. The shapely form of a woman stands at the cell door, silhouetted by the light from the corridor windows.

'I've been expecting you, gentlemen.' The voice has the soft melody of an educated English refrain. Her attire was simple, a cotton shirt and long shorts and revealed a woman who could handle herself, a scrubbed pale face, smiled beneath tightly combed black hair. Alluring hazel eyes surveyed the trio from behind a large pair of tortoiseshell spectacles. 'Mr Akash, Mr. Littleton & Doctor Hackney, I am glad to make your acquaintance; we have much to discuss, and it won't be long before they come looking for you here. Follow me, please.'

She spins around and leads them along the corridors. They follow, including Professor Saunders, who has now donned a large battered pith helmet and is now looking every bit the part. As they made their way through the Asylum behind their

mysterious guide, they passed the various cells and rooms
containing the poor, unfortunate souls incarcerated within.
Some of whom grin at them as they pass, others cower at the
appearance of strangers. Most just stare blankly with
indifference.

Presently, they arrive at an office. It is neat and practical. The
bespectacled lady takes up a seat behind the desk. Farouk,
along with Littleton and Hackney, all become more aware that
they are still disguised as native Arab women. Professor
Saunders, now smiling broadly at Littleton, looks away and
shifts uneasily at Saunders's unwanted attention.

The map that you carry, gentleman, was drawn by my father.'
'Your father?' Hackney replies, surprised. 'Then you must be
M.S.'

'Yes, I am M.S. It is I that sent
the disguises you now wear.'
'Disguises?' repeats
Professor Saunders,
looking again at
Littleton.
'What does the 'M' stand for,
Miss Saunders?'

Moppity
Saunders

Moppity.' Everyone repeats the word, except, of course, the professor, who must have become accustomed to his daughter's name by now as he had given it to her 29 years ago.

'Moppity - I like it,' Hackney says with a genuine smile.
'My father is the only man alive who can lead you to your goal. Between his odd bouts of, shall we say, strange behaviour, he is as sane as you or me.'

The men listen to her, not looking too convinced by her words.

'He remembers many things from his prior expeditions, and it wasn't until recently that he had an almost full recall of the events of 1907 and details of the events of his last abortive search for the Chantress of Asante.' She smiles half-heartedly at the professor before continuing, 'My father was a successful explorer, inventor, and businessman. His Empire was thriving, 'The Crackers of Kings'... I have waited years for the opportunity to pay back Bengay Wat for his betrayal and subsequent actions.' She spits on the floor at the mention of Wat's name.

The men listen attentively to her story.

'It was he who left my father as he is now. Those weeks of imprisonment beneath the desert sands took away a good deal of his sane mind. Do you know what he survived on, what he had to eat?' All three nod their heads.

Professor Saunders grins and nods at the three of them as they are captivated by the tale Moppity tells.

'Without my father, the business faltered, and things went from bad to worse. It was ultimately put into liquidation. It was eventually purchased by Lord Fern to become just another one of his many concerns. He kept the name, and every month, we receive a generous enough check that goes to the upkeep of this place. He turned the business around, and as you know, Saunders Crackers is now a very successful enterprise. He managed the enterprise and turned it around very well, and we are grateful that someone could. I have waited years for the opportunity to pay back that scum Bengay for his betrayal, and several weeks ago, that opportunity arrived.'
'Wat,' Littleton speaks aloud.
'I said, I have waited years to pay back that scum bucket of filth and betrayal.'

She spits on the floor at the utterance of his name again.

'While my father has declined, Wat has thrived. I had obtained a job in one of his bars without any suspicion on his part as to who I really was. I got a job as a waitress and was able to infiltrate this corrupt organisation. I know about the smuggling going on and agreed to help the SUTI as an undercover agent.'
'You are Monique from the Wandering Camel?' Hackney says aghast.
'And many others besides,' Moppity rasps the voice in the same huskily, disarming, sultry tone as the waitress had spoken.
'Good Golly,' Hackney can't subdue his surprise.
'I am with SUTI too!' exclaims Farouk. 'Yes, I know we have much to catch up on.' 'Go on with your tale Miss Saunders.'

'I received our regular cheque from England, with that cheque was a letter from Elizabeth Fern saying her father was now in declining ill health, along with details of your proposed expedition. She asked me to help. I knew you would need to talk to my father. We still don't know how he managed to escape the confines of the septic tank latrine, but he did, and that's all that matters. But he was found wandering more dead than alive, in the dry, hot desert. He had a map of which you have a copy. The reference points of which have never been deciphered until now.'

'About the map - we don't have it now. Bengay managed to steal it from us; he's a damn tricky fellow, as you know,' Hackney delivers this news to Moppity.

'Hmm I see... you have lost the freakin' map!' This news is certainly not what she wanted or expected to hear. Moppity takes a few moments to process a suitable alternative plan with her fertile and nimble mind.
'Hmm... maybe all is not lost. Everyone thinks my father is mad, but as I've told you, his recollections have been much clearer of late. We need him more than ever. He has made more recent copies. And together we have narrowed the area to within a few hundred yards. The keys to reading the map are decipherable. We're making sense of it, and recent developments have brought us to the point of almost one hundred per cent certainty that the Chantress of Asanti... lies here.'

She turns dramatically, pointing to a well-worn spot on the very large, antiqued, discoloured map of the deserts on the wall behind her. She rubs her finger over the spot.

'The Valley Where Everyone is Buried.' 'What's it called?' asks Littleton.
'That's what it's called, The Valley Where Everyone is Buried.'
'Oh, I see,' says Hackney.

'Mr. Farouk, if you don't mind working with a woman, I have details of our next move.'

'I certainly have no objections; you have shown yourself to be more than resourceful; together, we should be more than a match for Wat's villainous enterprise. I put myself in your capable hands.' Somewhat relieved to be 'relieved' of the position of having to know what to do. Farouk walks over to the map. 'You know for certain that this is the place we seek?'

'I know that if you look anywhere else, you will be digging your own graves,' she announces bluntly.

'We will need help. I have organised ten of my best orderly's. They have, in turn, picked out the most rational, sedate, and trustworthy patients available. In total, there will be over thirty of us, including yourselves. We leave tomorrow, and transport is arranged. Do you have any questions?'

'We will be stopped as soon as we set foot outside of here, they will be looking for us?' says Littleton with an uncharacteristic voice of warranted caution.

'They will be looking, but they will not find you, because you will not be with us. You, my friends, will remain here with my father. The sisters will look after you, and then you will take alternative transport. You will take a 'unique' alternative transport to our rendezvous.'

'Is it safe to go out with the Asylum inmates?'

'How safe have you been up to present, Mr. Akesh?' Farouk nods, 'Good point.'

'You and both your friends are quite safe.' She assures him.

'Point taken, it can't get much worse. If only I had read those briefing notes, I'd have been a little more on top of things.' 'So, we are to proceed out of the gates of the building with the expedition and the Asylum inmates?' quizzes Littleton. 'Will that not look a little odd?'

'Odd? Not at all; we do it all the time on field trips. It is an ideal therapy and an excellent cover; you will learn more later. Meanwhile, I'll let Sister George show you to your guest quarters.'

The kind-looking lady who had beckoned them in from the gatehouse appeared smiling.

'Come with me; you must want to change out of those clothes; you may start to like them, and that wouldn't do at all, would it?' Chuckling to herself, she leads the way from Moppity's office.

Chapter Nine
The Journey

That night they all slept like babies and convened for breakfast in the early hours of the next day. Hackney even found some sugary breakfast cereal and treated himself to two helpings.

'We are ready for our journey and we must be off the compound within the hour,' a confident smile flashes across Moppity Saunders's face.

Today, she bore no resemblance to the bespectacled vision of yesterday; she looked different, almost unrecognisable to the eyes of Littleton, Hackney and Farouk; her confidence was infectious. Over breakfast, details were finalised, she was very much in charge, and things were beginning to get done. Wheels had been set in motion and it looked unusually as if someone might know what they were doing.

The rest of the expedition crew would consist mainly of inmates and orderlies.

'I've dressed everyone in white linens and hats. Each person has a large number written in black ink on a card pinned to the front of them. They work much better if they know they are part of a team, which makes it easy to identify and organise.'

'Which ones are the patients?' Littleton enquires.

'Oh, we have no rigid set of rules here, sometimes they swap over. The inmates swap places with the orderlies and the orderlies with the inmates; it makes for variety. Sometimes, those who are doing the locking up, like to be locked up themselves for a little peace. So, it all will work out fairly and squarely by the end of the week. After all, this is a lunatic asylum.'

'Yes, it is,' Littleton adds absentmindedly as he watches an inmate painting a cat in the exercise yard beyond the open window. The animal struggles and will need his matted fur washed thoroughly with soap and water later...

'And we are very forward and progressive in our thinking, in our modern ways.' She takes a moment to look around her as if someone may be listening, 'We must arouse as little suspicion as possible, as even now, there are forces massing against us, watching our every move. I've arranged a little deception that should work to our advantage. You will not leave here with us, but later this evening with my father. I rather think that as soon as we step foot outside the gates, we will be stopped and searched. Koresh and his men will be looking for you, but needless to say, they will not find you. You can hide here, the order of sisters that take care of the patients here are loyal and true. No man from the outside can enter this house unless he has been deemed nutty as a fruitcake.' She smiles, 'I have also spread the rumour that we have had an outbreak of Watumba number-two fever, a very contagious disease that affects the nether regions and various parts of the garden.'

'How do you plan we should leave here? When do we? And which way do we go? We've been given no directions or instructions,' Farouk inquires.
'This is the rather exciting part for yourselves. My father will lead you out of here by one of the many tunnels that run as far as the Tetsi watering hole.'
'Tunnels, Tetsi?' Littleton, along with Hackney, indeed, all three are becoming a little more skeptical of Moppity's plans.

'Yes, the soldiers of the Napoleonic War era were garrisoned here many years ago, beneath what was once the stockade. A large tunnel was found that was used to escape certain death of a court-martial verdict, and the bullets of a firing squad. It was dug by the imprisoned men and used on more than one occasion for their future escape. We will meet at the Tetsi. My father and Sister George will take good care of you.'

With that, she clips the oxen's reins and the animal begins to move between the yokes of a heavily loaded cart stacked with equipment. The wagon train trips out to the courtyard, followed by several others, each loaded with happy lunatics smiling and numbered. Littleton even gets a wave from an excited number seven. Half-heartedly he smiles as best as he can and waves back.

They watch the troop leave the confines of the Sanatorium Lunatique - pondering their next move. The professor lingers, smiling beside them, his hands gripping the braces of his trousers.

'Do not be too disheartened, gentlemen. I have another surprise for you; follow me.' The professor shows no sign of any insane dementia or infirmity but is calm and confident.

As they make their way across the courtyard, he elaborates on his surprise.

'Like my models, I build working machines full-size. At my factories, my machines and inventions produced crackers and biscuits by the tens of thousands. Extruding all sorts of shapes and complicated concoctions. Whole wheat, lightly salted, water biscuits, and table crackers, along with my biscuit-butter crumbles.... every hour of the day. I employed technology way ahead of its time. Well, I have refined that technology and harnessed its potential - taken it to its third dimension, you might say. What you are about to see may astound you. People might say it's way ahead of its time. People might say what is it? But I spent my time wisely, the fruits of my labour will enable us to leave here completely unnoticed: practically invisibly.'
'It's not a beetle, is it?' asks Littleton.
'Come with me, and I'll show you.' The professor leads the way.

They all troop across the hot, dry courtyard towards a single-level building that looks to be a warehouse of sorts. After entering through a large wooden bolted door, they follow Saunders down some dusty steps into the coolness of a spacious basement. He flicks a light switch, and everything is revealed more clearly. An expansive canvas tarpaulin covers an indiscernible object, the professor's latest model.

The men stare at the covered enigma beneath the sheet. There is an air of anticipation and the faint smell of cabbages.

'What is it?' asks Farouk, as all three start to wonder if it was the best of moves to stay here with the professor. The professor is showing extreme signs of excitement as he holds the edge of the tarpaulin, gripping it tightly with both hands, the object beneath causing him to slightly salivate. Then, with the nimble theatrical gesture of a Broadway magician, he whips back the dust sheet to reveal ...
'Gentleman, I give you the Desert Rover!' 'The Desert Rover?' they all gasp!

The men stare at the weird, but interesting contraption, revealed before them. Many spring-topped valves and tubes of shiny steel festooned with intricate piping, coupled to gauges and wheels, cylinders of polished brass reflect their mesmerised faces of astonishment. There is a cockpit of sorts, not dissimilar to a rudimentary motorcar and leather cushioned seating atop the caterpillar-tracked, mechanically odd vehicle. The cockpit has leavers and controls on a raised polished wooden console, with a buttoned captain's seat for the driver and pilot.

'What is it, though, professor?' Hackney is genuinely puzzled.

'It, gentleman, is our transport. It has taken me many years. Tonight, she will live and breathe; she's a beauty, alright,' he runs his hand over a polished panel.
'Yes, but how do we get the Desert Rover out of here?' asks Farouk.

The vehicle in question is the size of a more moderate horse carriage and looking to weigh more than a ton. It looks too large to get out of the door and weighs the better portion of a modern armed tank.

'Out of here? Why we don't need to get her out of here? She will take us under there.'

The professor gestures to a large set of shelves and empty boxes that are set against the wall directly in front of the Desert Rover. Saunders bids the men to help him move them. Once moved, the old tunnel that the professor and his daughter spoke of becomes evident. The machine looks as if it will just about fit along the rough-hewn tunnel walls.

'This is amazing, professor. What does she run on?' Hackney quizzes the professor.
'She runs on steam or, to be more precise, dried camel dung; the methane content of the highly combustible and readily available fuel is perfect for our needs. The fuel is contained in here,'

pointing to a door on the rear of the strange vehicle. He unlatches the compartment and then grimaces, waving his hand in front of his face. 'Pooweee... Perhaps not quite as dry as we'd like it to be, but soon it will be a fine fuel.'
'Camel-poo propulsion by-jove whatever next?' Hackney quips.

As darkness falls, the four men prepare for the upcoming journey.

'The Tetsi watering hole is about twenty miles due east, the first couple of which we shall travel under the ground. Just as a worm might. Now, take your seats, gentlemen. I must prime the primers and set the console collaborators to the correct calibrated positions required for the journey.'

A large, wooden-handled hand crank is inserted into a slot, which he turns slowly at first, getting more vigorous as the compression starts to build. The machine starts to give off some coughs and gurgles, and a little smoke appears from one of the many exhaust pipes. Smaller valves start to open and close in unison, and then larger ones follow. A tiny part of the engine seems to start up and then, in turn, encourages another and then another until the machine is alive, breathing, pulsating. The basement begins to fill with steam and the smell of its fuel.

'Wow,' all three of them are in disbelief that the contraption actually runs like a fine timepiece.

'Odds bodkins!' Hackney exclaims.

'It's almost ready, the rayonic dispenser has to warm to a temperature of 85 degrees. Then the other parallel converters will come online to spark in sequence, of course; once the dispenser is warmed up and locked into the under-dangling ionic strength inverter, we can begin our journey.'

The men are rightly not understanding a word of the professor's technobabble.

'I would, of course, I would have used an over-dangler, but as you can well imagine, it is so difficult to get the parts out here.'

He ushers them aboard. Each man has a face that belies their admiration for the professor's now burbling invention. The professor takes his seat alongside the men. He begins to shout at the top of his voice, as the machine is now rather loud in the quietness of the damp room. He points to a small line of lights set on a brass plate within the console.

'When this set of lights glow, as they are doing now, I release this handle thus and we will be off!' The lights began to glow brighter. Each man was now gripping the handrail provided, expectantly unsure as to what may happen next.

Momentarily, the lights sequentially glowed brighter then blinked, the professor released the leaver with a click and they were off.

The distance was picked out by two powerful electric carbon arc fuse lights on the front that provided illumination with the aid of large reflective magnifying lenses. The Desert Rover slowly picked its way into the tunnel. Bumping along slowly at first, but as the professor unleashed more of its power and steam, it began to move faster on its tracks; gradually, as the professor began to pull back the long brass lever, it was able to pick up more speed. The rover was breathing steadily like an unleashed animal of great power!

Professor Saunders was in his element, fully at ease in his helmet, beaming a confident smile as he set about adjusting and fine-tuning the controls in the instrument console.

Beset with flashing lights and moving gauges that he twiddled and repositioned up and down while mumbling to himself. Farouk sat up front with him while Littleton and Hackney were content to let fate pass them in the rear.

The tunnel floor was angled downwards for several yards, and the gradual slope levelled off the further they went. The walls were now dry and smooth, strengthened and supported further by timber beams, a recent addition to the excavation.

Everyone was enjoying the ride as each took turns stoking the boiler with the dried camel dung pieces. The Professor steered his contraption and concentrated on the controls. After about twenty minutes, he slowly eased back on the throttle as the tunnel gently began to angle upwards on a slight incline.

'How do we get out?' asks Littleton, looking around and shouting above the noise of the machine.

'Wait, watch this... ' Professor Saunders leaned from his seat, arm outstretched, his fingers finding what he was looking for.

The Professor pressed a small rock that seemed oddly out of place on the otherwise smooth surface of the tunnel wall. A click, then a heavy grinding sound rumbles around them and in the distance, a large slab of rock moves to reveal a night sky full of stars. Once more, they are now moving faster as the Desert Rover picks up speed, it leaves the confines of the tunnel and is coughed in by the coldness of the desert night. The grinding slab of stone moves back into its original position behind them. The seemingly barren sand has given birth to the Professor's wondrous contraption.

'The Desert Rover, what a machine! I knew she wouldn't let us down,' the professor beamed with the pride of a proud parent at the performance of his finely tuned creation. All three men are greatly impressed by the professor's skill, wondering how they could have doubted him. The vehicle was proving remarkably adept. It trundled beneath the desert sky, billowing smoke and steam from various pipework. Whilst maintaining a steady lick across the sandy terrain.

'We should rendezvous with the others within the hour at this speed, the encampment should be just around the next set of dunes,' he shouted above the noise of the rover.

It had all gone better than expected... up until this point. The rayonic converter, unfortunately, was now warm to overheated and was to become a factor in the speedy and unplanned dismantling of the Desert Rover.

An odd, offbeat, out-of-place, un-rhythmic knocking noise starts to intermittently shake the vehicle. A sound that was out of place in what had before been an otherwise finely synchronised beat of steady well-oiled engine tones.

It grew louder and more worrisome as the professor began to wrestle with the controls. The vehicle started to vibrate and judder uncontrollably. A loud bang goes off beneath them, and the sound of springs uncoiling, smoke, and then flames appear and start to lick around the workings in front of the professor.

The flames are spreading rapidly but still; the steam machine keeps on blindly.

Just as they rounded the last dune, as the professor had said-lay the torches and fires of the encampment they were due to join. The professor's daughter and the rest of the inmates from the Asylum now watch eyes agog as the speeding fireball that is picking up speed, it hurtles towards them. The burning remnants of what was once the professor's proud creation was heading for the largest tent.

The speeding fireball, which was formerly the Desert Rover, approached the tents despite the professor's frantically best efforts to stop it. A particularly watchful group of numbered individuals gathered to stare blankly at the rapid approach. To the horror of those aboard, it looked as if it was indeed a forlorn effort; the end was in sight.

The fastest of the watching numbered individual men begin to race in various directions from their vantage point.

Successively, each tent caught fire as flames from the Rover passed it, leaving only a large white tent in the path of the now apparently out-of-control approaching fireball.

The fireball entered the large tent. The expansive sleeping quarters of most of the helpers and inmates - it does little to slow its forward motion as it careers blindly. None of the four men aboard were able to see anything, especially being unable to see the large palm tree in its path. All aboard jump as if pulled to safety by an unseen drawstring. A tumultuous crash of bending metal and breaking pipework fills the night air. The huge bang of a collision rocks the palm tree, knocking several coconuts to the sand.

Then, silence for a moment, apart from the burning tents and mayhem around the camp, all is quiet.

Steam hissing and water showering out under pressure punctuated the night air. The fire, after a few minutes, extinguishes itself, and slowly, the passengers emerge from the devastation and darkness. The speed and the impact, fortunately, were reduced by the soft sand. The wreck is thankfully not serious enough to cause any major injury. But the Desert Rover has roamed her last and will never roam again.

They stagger from the wreck one by one from the twisted metal and hissing steam. The professor looks over the debris field - a man in a trance. Another in a palm tree.

'Bugger... '

'It appears that the Rover had a minor design fault that I shall have to rectify,' he stammers.

The professor's daughter, Moppity, has pushed her way to the assembled crowd, who stares blankly at the new arrivals.

'What happened?' she asks despondently.
'We've had a bit of an accident,' the professor moans as he rubs his head.
'The encampment is destroyed, father... ' 'Sorry about that, my dear... '
'Well, at least you have survived. Now you've arrived, is everyone alright?' Ascertaining by shaking arms and slapping legs that they are still of sound body, at least.
'We will have to work out new sleeping arrangements, seeing as you seem to have trashed yours and several other people's quarters.'

Surveying the remains of the smashed Rover, now laying on

its side like a mortally wounded dying dinosaur, swathed in tent canvas, the charred and smouldering remains of what were the well-prepared tents and blankets that were to have been the sleeping arrangements for the night.

Things gradually settle down. Around the glow of the warm campfire, Professor Saunder's Moppity, introduces them to number one and through to number twenty-two by way of the large handwritten numerals displayed on the front and back of each helper and former inmate of the Sanatorium Lunatique.

'As I expected, we were stopped by Koresh and his men. They were more than disappointed not to find you. Mr. Littleton, you now have a reward on your head. The man you shot was a cousin of Bengay. It may have been a mistake to leave a loaded firearm in your keeping.'
'It was an accident.' Littleton says adamantly.
'Didn't they recognise you as Monique?' asks Hackney. 'Of course not, I can be very convincing ... ' in her spectacles, she speaks in an exaggerated sweet tone
impression of herself denying any knowledge of the English men that Koresh is searching for, and then she switches effortlessly to the dusky, heavily accented voice of Monique, the curvy waitress from The Camel. As a voice artist and actress, she is completely convincing.

'Wow, good gracious and odds bodkins!' Hackney is rather impressed and charmed again. 'Hang it all if I say you are a devilishly talented woman Ms Saunders, a proper actress, you should be on the stage.'

Moppity brushes aside Hackney's gushing compliments. 'After you have eaten you can make use of the spare tent, we will go over the plans again tomorrow. I'm tired now; I'll see you in the morning; I still have much to do in preparation for tomorrow.'

She bids the men goodnight and retires to her tent for the night. Leaving the three new arrivals around the fire with several of the inmates. The other's eyes are glazed and fascinated by the fire's embers fanned by a light, desert breeze that has sprung up and dances over the flames. So, the eventful day closed with scout songs around the fire. Numbers 1 to 7 surprise everyone with a rather slick shimmy shuffle sand-dance accompanied by the intermittent groans of an injured cook, whom someone had taken issue with for his use of tarragon in the evening meal.

The morning dawned, the first morning of the expedition proper. Everyone had given their commiserations to the professor regarding the demise of the Desert Rover. Who mumbled something about some over-expansion of the ionic converter, something he would rectify if he ever got around to building a replacement model.

Moppity appeared at breakfast, striding from her tent with a camel riding crop, dressed in a long-flowing linen dress, a large wide-brimmed shady hat, tied with a gauze scarf neatly beneath her chin. Her transformation does not go unnoticed, especially by Hackney.

'I say...'

She briefed everyone over breakfast, conferring with the professor, who still retained commendable knowledge, that made it easy to forget his hitherto recent previous rent-free address.

Their journey would take them to the little village of Biloxi. The mountain village was built in approximately the same geographical position as the ancient Asante Temple. It was a full day's journey from the Tetsi hole. Several reluctant camels and carts with a few oxen were loaded with supplies and the camp was dismantled tent by tent.

Sat in front of the less cluttered carts, about halfway down the procession, Littleton and Hackney perched on the bar seat, surrounded by equipment and several cages of very lively chickens. Farouk travels behind them, with two smiling members of the help. Camels and carts loaded with supplies and provisions, along with crates of equipment, waited to begin the journey.

The signal to move out was given, and the motley troop got underway to begin its meandering trek along the desert track beneath the brightly beating sun.

The previous night's encampment was packed and disappeared over the sand-dune horizon, leaving barely a sign that anyone had been there. Except for the extensive fire-burned wreckage of the Desert Rover now resting on its side against the oddly leaning charred, still smoking palm tree. Camels and oxen made complaining noises as they left the scene to trundle along loaded with the supplies that the dust and sand would permeate extensively over the course of the journey.

The sandy expanse of the horizon was bathed in the warm air that would flow from the south, sometimes creating desert mini-tornadoes of rising sand that would now and again descend on the troop like dusty dervishes. Everything seems out of focus in the glowing haze of incessant heat, shimmering and hot.

After a few miles, it became evident that Hackney was getting on famously with one of the chickens. Littleton watched as his friend took the bird from its cage and let it sit on his knee, gently stroking its feathers. Talking to it as if it was a small child. Whereupon the chicken would warble happy chicken noises; as we all know, chickens are a lot more affectionate

and more intelligent than we give them credit for. Littleton, not
wanting to come between a man and his bird, turned to watch
the mauve sandy desert gently rolling past.

He thought back to his childhood ambition fostered as a young
boy to one day discover anything famous and have people say
his name and think of the great explorers.

Littleton, great discoverer of things... Larry Littleton great discoverer of ancient things. He thought of a pretty young girl he had once known who visited the house in his childhood... The way she had made him feel as a young boy and how strangely he was reminded of her at this present moment, along with the strange set of circumstances that have led to their present predicament.

'What did you say?' questions Hackney. Littleton jumps back into reality with a shudder, and he is again back on the cart travelling through the desert heat with Hackney, Farouk, and a friendly chicken.

'Oh, nothing, just talking to myself, I expect.' Littleton replies dreamily.

The long sandy stretches before them were occasionally interrupted by a lush green pasture or a rich swathe of cultivated land. White egrets stood stone still in the irrigation ditches whilst rust-coloured hawks flew overhead as tiny yellow birds settled on the backs of the grazing cows and water buffalo. The late afternoon becomes old, and the lead car with Moppity and Professor Saunders circles off the track. With a wave of her hand, she indicates that they are approaching the destination. The little dwellings of the village of Biloxi are coming into sight.

Houses built of sun-dried bricks and pyramids of hay or drying animal dung are tended by turbaned villagers. It is time to make camp.

The assortment of tents and carts and wagons grind to a stop and begin to unload. A herd of camels approaches and crosses between Littleton and Hackney's cart. They wait as Littleton looks on at a large female beast, loaded with a few blankets, meets his gaze and approaches. Both stare at each other; the camel frowns before drawing back her lips in what seems like a toothy smile. She then sends a powerful jet of saliva, spitting with uncanny accuracy into Littleton's face. With that, she moves off as if nothing had occurred. Littleton sits stony still, not even flinching at the yellow frothy saliva that dangles from his face and chin. The frothy pale cream-like substance drips slowly from his resigned but seething features.

'I'd read they do that,' Hackney says as he reaches into his pocket and hands Littleton a handkerchief to wipe himself off.

Tents are rigged simply and effectively, except in Littleton and Hackney's case where just simply was used. A large fire is made up in the centre of the gathering; several iron pots are suspended from triangular constructions to be heated above the flames of the charcoal fires as dusk falls.

The cook is an uncommonly filthy character, with a limp from the previous night's injury sustained in an encounter with a disgruntled customer approaching. He sets about the task of preparing the evening food. The two men watch as he makes his way toward them, shiny meat cleaver in hand. Smiling, he takes the crates containing the chickens, including the one that Hackney had become rather fond of. Hackney defiantly grips the cage and tries to wrestle it from the cook's grasp. The cook hardly flinches and pulls the cage closer to him as if Hackney was merely an irritating fly and wasn't pulling it at all. He's, at first, unwilling to relinquish his grip on the cage, and the cook pulls him closer to within inches of his unshaven, coarse features. Hackney lets go as he smells the heavy spice-laden breath of the cook and relinquishes the cage.

'What's for dinner? Littleton asks.
'Duck stew,' replies the cook.
'Well, there's no need to be rude, at least it's not chicken, eh,
Hackney?'
The cook laughs and holds the cage up in front of him as he
walks back to the makeshift kitchen.' ... quack, quack, quack,'
the cook sneers, mocking Hackney further by making the sound
of a duck. Littleton smiles at Hackney half-heartedly as he
attempts to be of some comfort by patting him on the shoulder.
'I'm not hungry,' Hackney says, watching the cook disappear
behind some crates with his chicken.

A frenzied squawking arises from the highly stacked crates -
silence, then a few feathers rise into the hot desert air, one of
which floats and flutters in front of Hackney's tearfully
disappointed eyes.

Chapter Ten
The Dig

At this very moment, what could loosely be described as the Fern expedition is being watched by the unseen eyes of another interested party.

From the cover of the two shady date palms, by the furthest dunes a quarter of a mile away, a pair of powerful binoculars are tracking the proceedings. The beautiful, but ruthless daughter of the one they call the Black Scarab. Sonia Sinclair lowers her set of double-coated Zieca-lensed binoculars and smiles. She is dressed as a local, sitting side saddle on a groomed camel. A large, hairy single-hump dromedary, surrounded by several of her men, looking like something from an exotic chocolate confectionery commercial.

'You have a powerful-looking pair of binoculars,' one of the attendant men says mistakenly, as he tries to strike up a friendly but ill-conceived conversation.

'If any man so much as thinks of laying a finger on them,' she pats the equipment on her chest, 'I'll slit his throat from

ear to ear.' She gestures by slowly drawing a finger around her throat without looking at the man who had paid her the compliment.
'Yes, ma'am, it is understood, ear to ear,' he says quickly, retreating from her presence to a less conspicuous position.
'Now, I don't know what funny business is going on here, but somehow, our four pigeons have managed to escape the confinements of the Asylum and have joined the others.'
'We must infiltrate the camp tonight and slip a little something into the food,' she turns her head and shouts, 'Abdul!'

A dark and foul-smelling creature answers her call, twitching his curious features. He is a big, bony fellow with the countenance of an ape, only perhaps less intelligent.
'Now, Abdul, you look convincingly like a lunatic, more so than anyone else, come to think of it, more so than anyone from the Asylum. We need someone on the inside, can you cook?'
'Cook what?'
'Food, you idiot?' she snarls.

Abdul smiles.

'Yes, if we or rather you, provide the food, it will be much easier to add some 'special' ingredients. Do you understand what I'm saying?'

Abdul gives every impression of understanding as he continues to smile, but then shakes his head in non-comprehension.

'A sleeping draft into the ingredients of their evening meal, we need to drug the food.'
'Ingredients?'

At this point, Sonia dismounts gracefully from her one-humped charge and approaches the apprehensive Abdul, frowning. Standing beneath a large, immobile Abdul, she draws back her lips and speaks menacingly slowly.

'Go and drug the people. Over there.' Pointing to the encampment from the Asylum, 'Find yourself a number to blend in with the others and get to it. We will wait until this evening, but for now, we will keep our distance. We will mix the sleeping draft and you need to make sure that they take it.'

****

The next day breaks and sunlight streams into the tent from the open venting. Hackney has slept a sound and solid sleep on his simple but comfortable camp bed. Littleton, on the other hand, has had a fitfully restless night.

He had dreamed vividly that in the darkness of night, he went to the watering hole to fetch water, and, armed with Hackney's pistol, he had run across Bengay. He dreamt he had fought a furious fight and killed the man and his monkey. It was hideous and so real.

'I had a bad nightmare last night, Hackney, old man, hideous it was and so very real.'
'Oh?'
'Yes.'
'That's funny, I dreamt about that filly we are avoiding, Sinclair's daughter - she keeps popping up, even though she is a rum version of a woman I'd say. Can't seem to shake her from my thoughts though.'

Shaking off the trauma of his nocturnal visions, Littleton rises and stretches his arms out to the new day. Stepping outside the tent, half expecting to see Bengay's bullet-riddled body drying in the sun on the warm sand.

He did not realistically expect to see the camp that they had previously retired from last night. The one that was now no longer there. Theirs was the only tent. They were alone: abandoned. Where was everyone? Littleton retreats into the tent and gets back into bed, pulling the covers back over his head, moaning in the hope that he is still dreaming.

Wishing that he is still dreaming; unfortunately, he is not. 'Hackney, take a look outside will you, old chum?' Hackney, registering the concern in his friend's voice, pulled back the tent flap.

Hackney and Littleton survey what was last night a bustling campsite. There were no carts, tents, or people, just the fire ashes and some ominous dark, dry blood stains on the sand. The cook, Abdul and his deadly ingredients had done their job. 'What do we do now? We're in the middle of the desert without a clue? No map, no food, no water, no breakfast, left to rot.' Littleton spins around madly in his nightgown before sinking to his knees, believing they are doomed.
'Why would they leave us here?' asks Hackney. 'Yes, why indeed?'
'And where is Farouk, this is all very strange,' he pops in a gobstopper absentmindedly. His brow furrows, pointing to a spot over in the distance.

'Stranger than we might think. Look over there.'
Hackney points to an upturned feed bucket moving along in the sand, pulled by unseen strings. Littleton and Hackney stand perplexed. What can such magic mean?

Hackney reaches into his pyjamas and pulls out the Ely number seven, which he has taken to carrying at all times. Outstretching his arm, taking careful aim at the bucket, he fires off a shot with uncanny accuracy. The impact blows it a few feet into the air with a deafening ricochet.

'A chicken!' they both repeat in unison.
'It's only a chicken, thank heavens! It was trapped under the bucket; come here, girl.'

Slightly dazed, but seemingly no worse for wear, the chicken meanders towards them.

'If only she could speak, we would know what happened.' He picks up the bird, who seems pleased enough to see him as he cradles the bird in his arms. 'Still, we are forgetting one thing, we still have the map.' 'No, we don't.' Littleton reminds him. 'Yes, we do.' Hackney counters. 'With the aid of the map, we'll know exactly where we are and where we must look.'
Littleton looks to be on the verge of tears as he stares skyward. 'The map from a madman? We lost the map back at the hotel, and Saunders hasn't had a chance to redraw
anything yet. Besides, where is he? Where is everybody? We are here alone,' Littleton drops to his knees.

'Steady on, old man; I'm sure we can find some clue here as to what has happened.'

'Well, I'm going home; I've had just about enough; look at this place; it looks as if there has been a battle here, and we slept right through it. Where is everyone? Why are we the only ones left?'

'And I wonder about the chicken; how did she survive?'

'That question may be about to be answered,' replies Hackney stroking the chicken and pointing it in the direction of an overturned cart around which lay the smashed provisions of the now disappeared expedition, broken equipment and shards of torn tent cloth.

But the oddest thing about the scene is the lone figure of a woman tied to the wheel of the overturned cart. A spark of recognition flutters within Hackney as they both approach the figure.

'It's Sonia Sinclair! Great-Scott!'

'Help me please... ?' she struggles with her bonds. 'Doctor Hackney, thank goodness... '

'Good heavens, what are you doing here, what's happened?' Her clothing is torn but intact, and they work quickly to free her, which is surprisingly easy.

'I was on my way to warn you that you were being duped, that Farouk and Saunders were impostors and that they were tricking you into providing them with Lord Fern's funds,

so they could steal any treasures that are found - should you two discover the Chantress. With my help and resources, we can move much more quickly... if you have the map.'

'Well, that sounds like the truth and a plausible way forward to me; what do you think, Littleton?'
'Wait a minute, Hackney, can I have a quick word?' He takes Hackney aside. 'This all seems very strange; where are the others? What happened to Farouk? We are the only ones

left... why is she really here? There is something fishy going on.' As they both turn around to ascertain the answers to these posed questions, their suspicions are confirmed. Sonia nonchalantly leans against the upturned cart, pointing what looks like Hackney's pistol squarely at them both. Hackney checks his pyjamas and finds his pistol has been taken out of his pants and is indeed now in her possession.

'She's whipped my pistol out of my pyjamas, Littleton. The hussy.'
'Have you no shame, madame?' Littleton says with an air of superiority in his voice.
'Shut up! I've had enough of this charade. I thought I would give it a try, but it is obviously not working. Give me the map now!' Sonia scowls, any pretense of camaraderie now gone.

'What map? We lost it back at the hotel; Bengay saw to that; we have nothing to give you.' Sonia turns and looks at the chicken standing innocently at Hackney's feet. Smiling, she lowers the pistol, aims, and then pulls the trigger of the Ely. The strike hammer hits the firing pin, and it goes off loudly with a resounding ricochet ... leaving just a pile of feathers where the unfortunate bird had been.

Hackney is incredulous... 'You, heartless fiend... you viper in petticoats... you... '

'Steady Hackney, we are British... ' 'Heavens, you're right, Littleton.'

'Let's keep our heads,' Littleton says stoically.

'I think you can see I mean business. Now the map or you are next.'

'What map?' Littleton repeats.

'The map Lord Fern gave you, now hand it over,' as she speaks her co-conspirators appear from the surrounding dunes and surround them. 'I think you have met Mr. Wat before,' Bengay staggered, awkwardly smiling a sickly grin. His monkey, Minki stares hard at Littleton in recognition.

Littleton shouts, pointing toward Bengay 'He has the map; ask him; he took it from our things at the hotel.'

'I hope they are not being difficult?'

'Oh, but they are being difficult,' Sonia smiles.

'I had hoped they might be,' Bengay does not attempt to hide his glee.

'Stop these pathetic lies. We found no map,' he says, looking in Littleton's direction.

Along with Bengay, it looked as if twenty or so men had appeared. There was no escape. The camels and supplies had been hijacked.

Littleton and Hackney stood pondering their fate as well as the rest of the other fellow group members now missing, along with all the inmates that had formed the ad-hock expedition.

The sun burned down hot, and their hearts began a rhythmic beat, getting a little faster as they tried to fathom the circumstances that confronted them. In the distance, a goat was heard to bleat soft and low.

'What happened to everyone. What have you done with Professor Saunders and Farouk?' Littleton addresses Sonia. 'Can't we all be friends? What's going on?' Littleton attempts a feeble negotiation.

'Well, seeing as you fell so soundly asleep last night, we thought it might be a good idea to orchestrate this little charade - but it seems to have been a waste of time - again, give me the map.'

'Where are the others? Littleton repeats.

'Mr. Wat, tell them,' she ushered, lighting up a cigarette. 'Since you ask, many years ago, when I was more legitimately employed. A certain professor and I discovered a large ancient empty sewage tank not far from this very spot...' he holds up an aged piece of discoloured paper. 'I even made a rudimentary map. My cartography is not up to much, but it serves its purpose as a guide. I left him there -although how he managed his escape is beyond me. This time he is joined by your friends and his meddlesome offspring. But this time, he will not be as lucky as to be able to escape, I can assure you.'

'You fiends!'

Bengay Wat laughs out loud as Sonia simply smiles.

'If you already have a map, why do you need another?'
'This is not the right map - the map you were given was copied from the Chronicles of the Cracker, the sacred texts are entirely different. The Chronicles of the Cracker has been sought and few have seen its recipes, but it also has another element of interest. It contains a very important, more accurate clue.'

Behind the two men unseen, two of the attendant thugs stealthily placed themselves ready to dish out Bengay's orders. They raised their arms high, bringing down two heavy coshes onto the hapless duo's craniums. Everything goes dim before lights out for Littleton and Hackney. The two men are coshed... unconscious.

****

Once again, the return to consciousness is reached via a long dark tunnel. They awake to find they have been tied and bound securely to a large tent pole. Both Bengay and Sonia are talking cross-legged on a comfortable rug, one of many laid out on the tent floor. Littleton feigns his unconscious state, keeping perfectly still, listening to the conversation of his two captors, his eyes tightly closed.

'So do not fail me, Bengay, this time you will do the job properly. These fools have no idea what is going on. They won't be missed,' Sonia speaks dispassionately between sipping her small dram of chai.

'Why didn't you put them underground with the others?' Bengay casts an eye over toward the two prisoners.

'The others can rest in peace for now. It is information that my father needs from these two.'

Littleton begins to get worried after hearing Sonia's words. What had become of those buried underground? He can only imagine their abstract fate.

'But we have searched for them, they have nothing on them. Why don't we just put them with the others and be done? It is cleaner that way. It will look as if the expedition got lost in a desert storm. You can report back to your father about the operation and all the loose ends have been secured. We will have no further trouble from the abortive Fern expedition; these desert storms can be lethal,' he smiles. 'The other explanation we could use would be the folly of their recruitment of the inmates from the asylum. If the storm didn't finish them off, then the mass attack of madmen would have. Who could disbelieve such a plausible explanation?'

Littleton winces at the words of his captors and is not reassured that they will make it out of their present predicament alive. Weighing all things up, he assesses the situation from a sly corner of one half-opened eye. He sees that he is near the edge of the tent and the two of them are tied behind a dressing partition that offers him some cover from the main part of the tent.

By furiously wriggling his feet in a bicycling motion, he is able to free his feet from their bonds. His binding did not secure him directly to the pole, and with some effort, he is able to move - but his wrists still remain bound. Flopping onto his stomach, he begins a maggot-like motion, a crawl across the tent floor to the wall, raising his stomach to force himself forward.

On reaching the hem of the tent where the canvas is not quite so taut, he is able to make a gap. Using his teeth to stretch the gap between the tent and the sand. First, he's able to force his head and then his shoulders through to feel the night air on his face. The sand around his lips is spat away with as much saliva as he can manage.

Lying half in and half out of the tent, he must make a dash for it as soon as he is able to stand. Wiggling like an irritated maggot, he leaves the confines of the tent behind him. Unfortunately, his activity has not gone entirely unnoticed -

he has attracted the attention of a prior acquaintance. One large female camel. The beast nonchalantly wanders over to where he is lying, Littleton lays perfectly still, hoping not to attract any further attention. Trampled by a camel? Is this the end? Will the beast pop his skull like a ripe watermelon or snap his limbs like brittle twigs in a forest of despair? The night is clear and starry, but is obliterated by the huge beast's belly as she stands over Littleton. His breath came in short gasps. He is rigid with fear.

Then it happens. From above his head, a torrent of hot water hits his face. Running into his eyes and tasting salty on his tongue. Running down his back and into his ears. It seems to go on forever. But luckily, a camel cannot urinate forever - one of life's small blessings. When it is through, the hulking beast moves off, leaving Littleton shaking, soaked and pissed on. He spits the best he can. The bitter lingering aftertaste of camel urine on his tongue is foul and sickly.

Littleton sighs and takes stock of his desperate situation; he can do nothing but carry on with his planned escape as he resumes worming across the cool desert sand. The stickiness of his urine-soaking causes the dry sand to adhere to him at the merest touch until he looks like an almost inhuman creation as he continues to awkwardly crawl away from the tent and gain more distance between him and his captors.

He would be back for Hackney momentarily, he told himself. His movements start to leave a clear trail that leads from the tent like a sidewinding serpent or a natterjack toad in the easily impressionable sand. It is this trail that Bengay's monkey, Minki, finds so interesting. The curious trail in the sand is what draws his attention as his inquisitive nocturnal wanderings around the encampment lead him to discover. Following for several paces, he picks up speed.

This easily followable trail that Littleton can't help but leave is the catalyst for his escape's ultimate failure. Following for several paces, Minki catches up with Littleton, now completely sand-covered and looking like a huge subterranean worm.

With an ear-piercing scream, the monkey signals the end to Littleton's desperate bid for freedom. The camp erupts at the monkey's alarm call and people rush from their tents to see what has aroused the little ape. Littleton lies motionless and empty as he hears his captors approaching, he awkwardly cranes his neck to view Sonia Sinclair, Bengay, and the monkey on his shoulder. All three laugh at Littleton's appearance and... smell.

'And where do you think you are going, Mr. Littleton?'

Littleton's heart leapt into his mouth as he lay staring at the tan suede safari boots of Sonia Sinclair; he contemplated the gold hand stitching and sighed, looking up into her cold, smiling face. You could see the Sinclair in her features. At that moment, he caught the family resemblance and her percentage showed in her icy smile.

'Not thinking of leaving us, were you? I thought you and the good Doctor Hackney had some discoveries to find. The Chantress awaits your successful unearthing, remember?' 'What have you done with the others?'
'The others are fine,' a voice said.

The new voice was Bengay's, and he stood somewhere behind Littleton, who by now was exhausted by his efforts and lay face down in the sand. He no longer needs to crane his neck.

'You are a more resourceful man than I took you for,' with that, she draws back her old braided safari boot and stands it on Littleton's head. It is more of a theatrical gesture that is meant to cause humiliation rather than pain and Littleton's eyes hardly water at all.
'Back to the tent!' she orders.
'We must think of something more restrictive for you two,' Bengay laughs out loud. 'Why don't we do what we always

do with troublesome captives?' They laugh together, the laugh continues into the night.

As morning draws near, the fresh day unfolds with new objects of adversity. Littleton and Hackney are both awake and now, indeed, reposing in a more restrictive situation. Buried up to their necks in the desert sands, unable to move a muscle, save for anything above the collar line. They had been planted some way from the shade of the tent. An unwanted aerial gang of feathered scavengers is starting to pay attention to the two heads in the sand. The soaring black dots of large winged Egyptian vultures circle overhead, the beating of their wings becoming more audible and unbearable the closer they get. They can feel the down draft of the bird's feathered limbs. One huge vulture lands first, taking up a watchful position only a few feet away from the two heads protruding from the sand. The first bird begins to walk awkwardly toward them, staggering like a man whose boots are too big as it closes the distance.

'Goodbye, old chum,' Littleton sniffs.

A trail of silver sand ants and a canal spider draw across the sand in unison for good measure. It truly looks like the end.

'Away, away!'

Strangely, it is Bengay who is their salvation. The startled bird takes flight.

'I hate those things. I have not finished with you two just yet,' he staggered towards the two seemingly disembodied heads; he was drinking from a large water can. Minki jumps down from his shoulders, likewise holding a smaller but identical water canteen. He takes a mouthful of water, then spits it into Littleton's face while sitting atop Hackney's protruding cranium. They both empty their canteens, wasting the precious water drawn from the well. Laughing, they head back for refills. It is a game in which they will not tire easily, but it is also one that will ultimately cost them their lives.

The monkey has been considered a filthy beast in certain cultures and less enlightened in more remote areas of the world since the dawning of the millennium. One such culture is the 'Bonan Bonee', a tribe of wandering nomads with a reputation for shooting first and asking questions later - well, they had some shooting to do today. As it turned out, this was about to be an especially bad day for Bengay and Minki, who had been drinking water from the well that incidentally was owned by this faction of the nomadic Bonee tribe. A tribe who today would have found it the ultimate insult for someone to let his monkey drink directly from the well.

By coincidence too, Sonia Sinclair is not the only possessor of a powerful set of binoculars. From a distance, unseen eyes have witnessed the trespass and transgression.

A faint rumble is heard in the distance, growing louder and becoming a visible sand cloud on the horizon, the sound of hundreds of trampling hooves. The nearest buzzard took flight as the approaching animals and faceless riders became more distinct. Surprised at the unexpected appearance of the strangers in an almost barren landscape, Sonia and Bengay, along with some of the men, stand motionless as they watch them approach. Everyone is transfixed.

It is a fatal mistake. The laughing stopped as the galloping riders approached. Bengay began to mouth something and turned too late. The report of a single gunshot was the last thing he heard as his life-less body tumbled face forward into the sand; perforated by a bullet to the forehead. Minki's eyes, bulging at what he had just witnessed, went wild as many more shots peppered the sand around him.

Miraculously, he evaded a direct hit and managed to scramble off between the crowd of the confused troupe, who were now trying to arm themselves and fight back. It is a hurried attempt to defend themselves, and each man tried to beat as plausible a retreat as possible. But under the relentless fire of the Bonan Bonee, it was useless.

The attackers had been tracking them for days as they watched the odd group led by the fair-haired foreign woman. Unable to do anything else, Littleton and Hackney watch the scene unfold before them from ground level or sand level. They stare with open mouths in disbelief as the scenario unfolds before them like a bizarre theatre show that they are watching from the balcony.

The largest tribesman heads for his goal; Sonia, who makes a futile attempt to run for cover, but to no avail. Seemingly without effort, he gallops alongside her, amused as a cat maybe with a mouse it is toying with; he quickly catches her and sweeps her up in his large, hairy arms.

'You'll never find the others without me; they will die!' she screams as she struggles, looking towards the two heads in the sand. The last thing they see of her is her flaying monogrammed boots, kicking wildly, showing her lace undergarments as she lay across the camel saddle and is ridden out of sight by the tribe of wandering, warring warriors.

A few moments later, the rest of her colleagues are either dead, dying or disappearing. The encampment is now fully ablaze and fully ransacked. Bengay lies dead, a single bullet wound to the head.

He has been joined in death by many, and Sonia Singleton's fate can only be imagined. Two heads of Littleton and Hackney craned in unison, unsure whether to make their presence known or not. But both think that a ray of hope may be implied in Sonia Sinclair's' parting words, 'They will die,' inferring that they were not already dead.

The chaos subsides and the bloodthirsty tribe departs and disappears over the horizon, leaving Littleton and Hackney to blister in the burning heat, like two red cabbages in a macabre arid garden.

So, without even getting one message home about their progress, they had now lost all hope of a rescue. As the minutes pass, the prospect of a happy ending dwindles further, who can now know their perilous predicament?

A certain pair of eyes would, and do. They belonged to a rather vengeful monkey who had taken refuge beneath an upturned wooden crate during the murderous fracas. He squinted with seething vengeful hate through the slatted planking from beneath a battered banana crate.
'I say, Littleton, do you hear that noise?' asks Hackney through chapped, dry lips.

Chapter Eleven
Rescue?

The faint drone of the tiny single-engine Belworth Ranger bi-plane was barely audible as it buzzed over the dry desert-scape, but it was there. The little, black spec in the flawless crystal blue sky grew bigger and became a bird, growing gradually larger as it approached until it was a recognisable aeroplane - a relatively new invention of the age. Flying low, following the contours of the undulating dunes, before it circled the two heads protruding above the sand. It was more than an unusual sight to see an aeroplane, especially out here in the desert. Especially for Littleton and Hackney, who had thought they would never say anything else ever again. The little plane circled, then dipped and began to lose altitude. The burble of the multi-piston engine grew louder as the flying machine neared the baking desert sand.

A proposed landing area was picked out by the pilot, one that looked suitable for the purpose. Sparsely populated with a few blades of saran grass with no particular obstacles to impede the wheeled skids. Touchdown and taxi were executed flawlessly.

Smoothly, the little plane bobs along the sand and is bought to within feet of the buried men's heads. The engine is killed and the leather-jacketed figure extracts herself slowly from the cockpit, silhouetted against the golden furnace orb of the beating sun. Confused and dazed, the two men look toward this new arrival, not knowing what to make of the aeroplane, or the mysterious lady aviator.

Friend or foe?

The rotund figure, a dark-eyed, plump, mysterious female with a broad smile, strides purposely from the plane. As she gets closer, she becomes recognisable. Standing before the immobile Littleton and Hackney, they survey the stitching of finely crafted boots. Looking up through sunbaked eyes, they gradually make out the features of Elizabeth Fern standing before them, not knowing whether to laugh or cry. Littleton smiles as best he can, his lips painfully dry.

'Lucky, you came when you did; we were just about to send you a wire,' he finds difficulty in speaking as the desert heat has dried all of his available saliva from his tongue, which is parched and swollen. 'To tell you of the expedition's progress.'

'The expedition's progress? What expedition?' she says, surveying the surroundings and their present predicament. She looks around at the smouldering debris of the camp and at Bengay's bullet-riddled fly- covered corpse, now baking in the sun, just a few feet away.

'How were you going to wire me?' she addresses the two immobile heads protruding from the hot sand like large animated cauliflowers.
'We erm ... would have sent a telegraph via ... ' none too convincingly, Hackney nods in agreement.

Elizabeth begins to remove her bulky, leather aviator clothing, a plus-size flying jacket with fur trim that is highly unsuitable for desert activity - once the cooling airflow through the cockpit is not available. A soft leather skull-cap, flying helmet and goggles are tossed to the ground, as is most of the cumbersome attire, now no longer of any use in the present baking environment.

'How did you know where we were?' asks Littleton's head.

'I didn't; it was luck, really; I made the journey by rail overland while Bessie,' she nods in the direction of the small aeroplane, '...was transported by freighter. Your trail was easy to follow. You seem to have caused havoc and mayhem wherever you have been. The police are keen to talk to you.

I gather amongst the many charges against you; you are also wanted for the murder of one of the local Police officer's brothers. If I were to discover your whereabouts, I am to inform them immediately. Have you actually managed to accomplish anything positive at all?'
'Well, I think that we... I think we will do.' Hackney again nods in agreement.

With a resigned sigh, she retrieves a small shovel from Bessie's cockpit and begins to dig out Hackney first, who, when free, in turn digs out Littleton. The sand was damp from their sweat, and their clothing clung to them, now cold and clammy. It was heaven to be awarded the use of their limbs again. The buzzards still circled overhead, this time with an eye on Bengay's mortal remains. From the privacy and shade of the parked aircraft, Elizabeth changed into the more sensible attire of a light gauze top, swapping her skirt for desert khaki shorts with sturdy boots.

After they were free from the sand's clammy grip, the three of them sat down to discuss the next move. Littleton stammered to ask the question that both men were thinking about.

'Before we go any further, Miss Fern.'
'Please call me Elizabeth,' she smiles disarmingly at Littleton.

'Yes, alright... well, Elizabeth, can I ask you why Hackney and I were chosen ahead of many others who were obviously qualified to look for the Chantress?'
'I think our present predicament illustrates admirably our unsuitability for the job.' Littleton's request cannot be ignored, and it is time for Elizabeth to level with the two of them.

She smiles and nods in agreement.

'Well, the truth is, Lord Fern, my father and your aunt, Lady Winterbottom, were once good friends. In fact, our pasts are very closely linked, Mr Littleton.'
'Oh,' slightly surprised at this news, Littleton now listens more intently.
'Or may I call you Larry?' Littleton nods, 'Yes, of course.'
'Do you remember a little girl you used to play with when you would visit the big house in Winterly Terrace as a child?'
'Winterly Terrace? Why, I haven't heard that name in years! Yes, that was a long time ago. Happy times, as I remember. The little rich girl who lived there, yes, I remember her.'
'And I remember you, brace yourself, Larry, for what I am about to tell you, as I was that little rich girl from all those years ago.'

The cogs begin to turn, and memories from the past of distant years come back slowly through the clouds of the years gone by...

'Not skinny Lizzy!?'

'The very same,' she smirks. 'How can that be?'

'I have put a few pounds on since then, as you can see - I have bloomed with the passing of years.'

'Yes, you have, but I meant, what are the chances our paths should cross again all this time later?'

'Do you remember the day I tied you to the railings and pulled down your britches?'

'Why no... well, yes, most embarrassing, yes.'

'Yours was the first Littleton I'd seen. Larry, you don't mind if I talk to you about the past?'

Hackney smirks at her story.

'Well, not really... it was a long time ago.'

'I know this sounds like a sort of madness, but I fell in love with you all those years ago. I made a promise to myself. I said I would never marry another man; I swore myself to you.' 'What?' gasps Littleton.

'It's true, I have been waiting for this moment, all those years ago I was a little girl... now I am well, I'm a big one. It was by chance that I found that you worked for Aunt Cynthia's favourite magazine. I persuaded my father, who has not been well, to stage the lottery. He knew nothing of Sinclair and his plan. I made you two the winners, and you won.' An almost coyish girl-like smile rounds off that last important revelation. Littleton catches a glimpse of the little girl he had known all those years ago.

'Why?' both question Elizabeth simultaneously.
'Because I intend to marry you and convince my father that you are worthy of joining the Fern family. I intend to take you up on your promise.'
'Promise?' asks Littleton, still in shock at her steadfast seriousness.
'Yes, I said I would never marry another man if you promised to marry me, and you did.'
'I was seven years old; surely you can't be serious?'
'Is the prospect that unappealing? Am I that ugly or too big for you now? Are you one of those fellows that just like skinny... birds?'
'Well, no, but I hardly know you. We hardly know each other. I was a little boy, and you were a little girl; we were just kids. It's just that it's a bit of a shock. Could I have a moment or two to think about it?'

Elizabeth lights up a cigarette. The golden kiss of the sun catches light beads of perspiration on her forehead; her cheeks glow with a healthy, rosy hue. Her features are indeed not unpleasant; she has a beauty and an air of refined breeding to her that the two men hadn't noticed earlier - plus, she can fly an aeroplane ... and she is rather posh!

'While you're thinking about it, also think about this: at home, you two are being feted as heroes for your fantastic discoveries and wonderful finds.'
'We are?' asks Hackney, smiling.
'Heroic, famed explorer engaged to the beautiful daughter of the Lord and heiress to the House of Fern, we are more than matched. My planning, although somewhat out of the norm, has paid off. Think about this, too: you were fired by your employer. What means of support do you intend to survive on after this is all over? You go back to your ordinary lives - they will seem frightfully dull, I can assure you, after all this adventure. And what's more, the Chantress of Asante is within our grasp.'
'She is?' skeptical at first, the two men are gradually falling under her spell.
'Well, that is what the rest of the world thinks. When we received no news from you, my father became very depressed and ill. So, I started to make stories up; one thing led to another; your dispatches that we received were filled with daring-do and laced with adventure.'
'They were?'
'The more fantastic your finds and adventures, the better his health got. The news seemed to act like a tonic, and by the

time I left for Egypt, he was looking better than he had done in years. He expectantly awaits our return. So does England. All the details I gave your editor, Mr. Jameson; he's been running the story for weeks. The whole country is gripped and following you as heroes.'

'Heroes, eh?' both now smiling smugly. 'But heroes for discovering what exactly?'

'The Chantress, of course, so we had better discover her, right?' Elizabeth says the last few words firmly.

'It's lucky for you that I came along when I did. It might have been curtains otherwise.'

Littleton looks and smiles with a little of something more than admiration in his voice.

'Yes, it's lucky you came along when you did. We are indebted, and I am indebted. Lizzy, may I call you Lizzy?'

'No, it's Elizabeth.'

'Yes, of course. Elizabeth. So, we seem to have had a few run-ins and setbacks since we last saw you, not least the loss of the expedition that we originally started with. Farouk, our guide, who is with the SUTI, by the way, has gone missing, probably dead - mainly all because of that foul fellow laying there, Bengay and his wretched monkey, Minki.'

Bengay was dead and accounted for; his wretched monkey

Minki, on the other hand, was not. And unbeknownst to the three individuals silhouetted on the desert sands. The vengeful eyes of Bengay's loyal primate were watching them. He had monkey madness on his tiny mind and a taste for revenge as he scampered across the hot sand toward the small, silent plane.
 Hopping on a wing spar and shimmying up one of the tension lines, he springs into the cockpit and drops from view unnoticed.

Elizabeth removes a thermos flask from her discarded flying jacket as they sit amongst the debris, unmoved by the sight of Bengay's still-warm corpse, so much so that Hackney drinks from the flask then rests it on the dead man's forehead right over the bullet wound as Littleton and Elizabeth watch rather disdainfully.

'Look at that. You can balance it on his nasty little head.' Hackney smiles, more than pleased with satisfaction at his act of disrespectful retribution against the dead villainous scoundrel.
'Wonderful, what a marvellous use for a cadaver; we could fold him up and use him later as a picnic table, maybe show respect, man. Remember, we must never lose our humanity; we are British; let's not forget that.'
'But he was going to leave us to die; he deserves no respect. But you are right, of course, King and country and all that.'

With that, he starts to go through Bengay's pockets.
'What are you looking for?' Littleton gasps, unnerved by the easy lack of respect for the recently departed Bengay.
'The map, he said, he had a map that he said showed where the others are.'
'Ah yes, good thinking, I was about to look myself.'

Hackney's rummaging pays off, and he produces a piece of torn paper that, earlier, Bengay had brandished in front of them. The map indicated a series of mounds on the horizon that were very close by and easily identifiable.

'Now we are getting somewhere,' Littleton gives a nod and smiles at Hackney's resourcefulness.

Meanwhile, in the cockpit of the Bellworth, someone else was about to get somewhere. It was in the cockpit that Minki, Bengay's now orphaned monkey, was pulling at wires and pressing switches in a vain attempt to destroy and sabotage the flying machine. The large red button marked 'starter' is hit forcibly and unmindful of any consequences. The button connected the ignition, and the still-warm engine responded easily and immediately coughed into life. Minki, panicked at the noise and vibration, began, quickly, frantically clutching at leavers and switches, inadvertently opening the throttle and releasing the brake. The now terrified monkey sat mortified as the plane moved and juddered forward and then began to pick up speed. Whatever he then did with his flaying, little hairy arms, fate contrived that nothing was to the detriment of getting the small plane off the ground. Terra firma was about to be left behind.

With a few bounces and lunges, the flat area of the desert surface that previously had provided a suitable landing strip now provided an equally adequate runway. The plane hopped once and then again and, just like that, was now fully airborne. At first, just a few feet, then increasing the space incrementally between the plane and the hot sand. The plane flew lopsidedly twenty feet or so above the sand, then quickly gained more altitude... lots more altitude.

'Wasn't that Bengay's monkey?' Hackney asks of no one in particular. 'I didn't know he could fly.'
'He's a surprisingly resourceful beast, that monkey,' Littleton adds.
'My Bessie!' Elizabeth gasps.

The three scrambled to their feet to watch as the little plane gained height erratically. The monkey's screams were drowned by the throb and burble of the twelve-valve 6-cylinder engine. As quickly as the plane had become airborne, substantial bad luck and gravity started to play their part in the downfall of Minki the Monkey's inaugural flight. Rising at breakneck speed in a vertical climb high above the desert until it was just a dot, the engine spluttered once, then suddenly stalled.

The black dot hung motionless for just a moment, suspended in mid-air, then gently turned earthward. The little dot became a bird and then a plane. A plane that was now heading from the sky toward the three of them at an alarming velocity. Whether Minki had learned the rudiments of aircraft control in his brief time as a criminal animal aviator or whether it was just plain luck, the plane now hurtled towards Littleton, Hackney and Elizabeth on a deadly dive of suicidal intent.

Everyone, without thought, scattered in different directions. The inevitable consequences of the plane's screaming downward trajectory were not actually witnessed by any of them, as each dived for cover to hide from the huge fireball that the exploding bi-plane erupted into as it smashed into the sand. Minki the monkey, Bengay's villainous cohort, again left this Earth for the second time that day. Propelled this time by aviation fuel and now in several disconnected monkey pieces. His villainous scampering days were now permanently over; he would be sick on no one else's shoulder ever again.

The three brush themselves off and stand to look out over the fiery, tangled, smoking scene.

'So much for using my plane to survey the area.' Elizabeth frowned as all three surveyed the smouldering crater on the very spot they had just been sitting. The crater that now contained the wreckage of the Bessie the Bellworth, pieces of Minki the monkey and underneath that, his bullet-riddled owner, Bengay Wat, the villainous scoundrel.

'It would seem that the Black Scarab's smuggling ring is losing a few of its key players.' Elizabeth muses. 'What of Singleton Sinclair's daughter? You mentioned her quite fondly in your only dispatch, which, if I remember correctly, told me how nice it was to be on a big boat with a porthole; you spoke of her as such distinguished company, Mr. Hackney'

Hackney shifts slightly, ill at ease with himself. 'I can only say that I made an error of judgment, as many men do over a damned attractive-looking woman.'
'She was trouble and would have left us to rot, I wonder what her position was in all this.'

He contemplates the dying embers of the wreckage of the plane. Littleton answers his question with a withering, 'I told you so' look.

'Well, she has a new position now, probably several new positions nightly, I shouldn't wonder, beneath that large marauding chap. The one that shot Bengay and carried her off has probably got a harem full of them she's probably just a number by now; that's what these chaps do; they are a rough bunch.'

Elizabeth pipes up, 'Well, that just goes to prove Miss Johnson wrong.'
'Who is Miss Johnson?' Both men enquire of Elizabeth.
'Our English teacher. I used to attend the same finishing school as Sonia. Stanford Girls High. She would always go on about Sonia Sinclair being 'the' Sonia Sinclair and being so successful a prodigy, how it was she that would obviously be the girl most likely to make it big. How wrong she was; teachers never get it right, do they?'

'Well, she wasn't far off, as she will probably be making it big every other night in some form or other as that fellow's plaything - pity really, as I think there was a spark of goodness in her.' Hackney says with a touch of melancholy in his voice.

Meanwhile, not two hundred yards away, hidden from view, was the entombed Fern Expedition secreted and sealed in the cavernous ancient first dynasty septic tank of Nephapu, the second or, as some say, Nephapu number two. All now incarcerated victims of the drugged chicken dinner, all unlawfully detained at Bengay Wat's pleasure. Unfortunately for them, Bengay was no longer with the living after he had met his untimely death at the hands of the marauding Bonan-Bonee. He was no longer available to avail himself of the proposed plans for the said detainees. They now languished in the confines of the dark tank.

Farouk had been the first to awaken from the drug-induced stupor, and he had organised numbers three, six, and seven to feel over the surface of the chamber to see if the weakness or fault might be apparent. The precious few matches that they had been able to scrape together gave them little comfort in their new surroundings. Rudimentary torches were cobbled together and shared amongst the expedition members who could be trusted with matches.

Inside the dark confines of the latrine tank chamber, the professor was facing his own demons as he remembered his first incarceration within the ancient septic tank many years prior. He shrugged off the deja vu and fought the irony of this, his second entrapment at the hands of Bengay Wat, as he tried to drag the details of his first entombment and subsequent escape from the back of his mind. He was somewhat reassured by the soothing words of encouragement from his daughter and number five and number twelve.

'If only you could remember the door, Father.'
'It will come to me, I'm sure; I'll have us out in a jiffy if only I could remember... there is a door.'

He tried desperately in the darkness to drag the details from the innermost recesses of his befuddled mind.

'That's it, that's it, a door! A door! Heavens be praised; we use the door to get in and out.'
'Yes, that's how we got in here, but they have sealed it up.'
'Have they?'
The professor is at a loss, the makeshift torches that they have put together are beginning to burn low, 'Wait! Wait, I have it now!'
The professor lifts himself to his feet gleefully. As if he has unlocked a great puzzle, he stands smiling.

'Yes, I remember now, I have to tap this wall from the top to bottom 1027 times, the same number of days in Nepherpu's reign. Then I whistled from precisely ten feet away, facing east, as the great winds of the Calamari had done on the day she died. On the day her mortal coil was called; there was a great passing of wind.'

Everyone went quiet. Number two giggled about the reference to passing wind.

'You are nuts, Father,' whispered Moppity beneath her breath.
'It's true, I tell you, that's how I escaped,' he smiles, 'it sets up a resonance you see within the wall - and the vibration acts like a sonic key. The tolerance is on the same syncopation.'
'I think the confinement may be affecting your brain again, Father. How did you count that many times, it would take hours,' she said.

'No, no, no, it won't. There are over twenty of us, and it will take minutes if we all tap 50 or so times each; we will be out of here in an instant, and you know how to whistle, don't you?'
'You just put your lips together and blow,' he smiles.
'All right, we've nothing to lose, we'll try it. Start tapping and counting.'

Everyone picks up something hard and begins tapping on the walls. Number 7 taps quite quickly, number 5 more slowly, and number 10 taps methodically. Number five's taps are barely audible as he is using a dried, dead mouse to tap, so his taps are much softer. Ten minutes later, Professor Saunders has been suitably slapped around the head and sent to the far corner of the chamber to be quiet. And keep any more of his stupid ideas to himself. 'And stop whistling!' somebody shouts.

Above ground, things are moving a little better toward the extradition of the expedition. From where they stand, Littleton, Hackney and Lady Fern can make out the simple, small white houses and shanties that make up the settlement of Bolloxi. The sparsely populated village at the entrance to 'The Valley Where Everyone is Buried.' Lady Elizabeth's quick-thinking mind goes into gear. She toyed with the idea of taking the fastest camel and eight strong men, then taking the strongest man and eight fast camels, or the muffled whining and braying of that unmistakable ship of the desert. A lone camel tethered to a palm made himself known. On closer inspection, it was found to be the irksomely troublesome camel that had plagued Littleton in the previous 24 hours. Remaining only in the vicinity because of her roping to a palm, which now swayed majestically above the waterwell in the slight breeze that had come up from the sands as you looked eastward.

On the trunk of the tree, they noticed for the first time a faded wooden sign with barely discernable script on its surface.

NOTICE: NO Monkeys, attended or
otherwise, to drink at the well
not now - not ever - this means YOU!
Signed the Bonan-Bonee.

Littleton squared off the camel's stare as the two eyed each other. Hackney, meanwhile, unhitched its restraint.

'We can't all ride him, Lady Elizabeth, you take the reins,' Littleton stands back as she confidently uses the reins to pull the camel's head and knees to the sand, before mounting the beast as easily as you would get on a bicycle. She is very good (and quite posh).

'Please call me Lizzy.' She relents.

With that, the three set off in the direction of the oddly shaped dune indicated on the map they had retrieved from Bengay's corpse.

The topography of the dune had an unnatural weld to it. Strangely hewn by the wind, it was a curious shape, an elongated nose, and at about the point of the nostrils would be a sand wall rose awkwardly to the crest of the nose's peak. Many empty discarded peanut shells told silently of a previous peanuty presence.

'I think we may have found something.' Elizabeth dismounts from the camel and the three start to dig at the spot where the peanuts trail ends abruptly in the sand. Sure enough, moments later, a door is discernable and the large stone slab that had sealed the entrance is visible. The words Nepherpu are read out aloud as Elizabeth deciphers the markings - 'This is the loo of Nepherpu! Nepherpu the second.'

She reads the words slowly. A faint knocking sound emanates seemingly from the stone inscription of the hieroglyphics. All three put their ears to the slab. There it was again, but louder. Scraping away the sand from the freshly sealed edges (that have not had time to set) and removing the camel jack from the toolbox with some effort, they prise open the would-be tomb. The door slab grinding on rough-hewn surfaces, gradually the heavy stone gives way, revealing many sets of beaming eyes in the darkness.

Farouk is the first to emerge from the darkness, shielding his eyes from the light; the others follow. The Professor and his daughter, who immediately strike up a conversation with

Elizabeth, they discuss the events that led to the present situation. They readily drink from the water canisters offered, which are retrieved from the leather satchels on the camel. The expedition is once more back on track; tired, thirsty, and hungry, but it is back on track.

Chapter Twelve

Organisation

Bolloxi is a small village settlement sitting above the entrance to 'The Valley Where Everyone is Buried'. It's a collection of primitive flat-roofed constructions with reed matting at the pane-less windows, worn wooden doors, and pastel-coloured shutters. Many wandering stray dogs take the shade where they can on any given hot afternoon as women sweep dusty steps with dry reed brushes.

BOLLOXI

The village's main source of income and sole significant business was to provide the archaeological digs and expeditions with manpower. Diggers, scrapers, sifters, and carriers and brushers. The most avidly read newspaper in town was 'The Daily Digger' in which Elizabeth had managed to place consecutive advertisements from England before she arrived in Egypt.

The Fern Expedition and search for the Chantress would pay a fair day's wage for a fair day's work. The ads have produced a good response. Many men are eager to feed their families and the wages the dig will garner are expectantly awaited. The only accommodation for those looking to be part of the expedition was a small hotel in town by the name of Bilious Bedouin: it was packed two to a bed with willing workers from around the surrounding valleys and deltas awaiting the arrival of the Fern Expedition.

And arrive it does. In the form of a sizeable and purposeful woman of substance, striding ahead of a rather stubborn camel, that has on its back two rather pathetic, exhausted characters in the form of a world-weary Littleton and Hackney, who had deemed that fate should do what it will with them, too tired and without the will to care anymore. The large, burly frame of Farouk strode behind the professor and his daughter, and then in single file, hands were on each other's shoulders, some with faces frozen in smiles, and the rest of the remaining expeditions were all numbered consecutively. A group of people could only be described as having an unusual appearance and disposition, and it was comprised collectively of the inmates of the Sanatorium Lunatique.

This was the Fern Expedition.

Thankfully, the supplies that had been organised had arrived at the hotel. A makeshift camp was set up just beyond the village perimeter and within the entrance to the valley. Tomorrow, the search would begin.

The morning's watchword is 'organisation,' the two, maybe three dozen or so men, that had applied in response to Lady Fern's advertisement in 'The Daily Digger' were mobilised as Professor Saunders goes over the map. The likely areas are highlighted and sectioned off. Larger maps are made and posted on makeshift notice boards within the quickly erected headquarters and around the camp. Areas are all allotted to small teams.

One of the smallest teams is comprised of Littleton and Hackney; they are given a G-section with a small foreign-accented fellow, Klause Hergashimer, who kept talking about the little people but eventually wandered off with his clipboard and pen. Leaving just Littleton and Hackney, who are both equipped with their trowels, sieves, and spades. G-section is, unbeknownst to the two of them, the least likely area to yield anything worthwhile, and so is also the area in which they can do the least harm, should their enthusiasm get the better of them.

A few hours into the dig, toiling below the hot desert sun, we find Littleton, poised motionless, bucket in hand, his quarry, a small brown spotted Lazarus lizard sunning itself on the baking sand. Holding the bucket rigidly in front of him, he lifts it higher and ever so slowly smashes it down on the poor creature, hoping to trap it beneath. Upon its successful capture, he would name the beast Lizzie. But alas, it was not to be. His prematurely twisted smile becomes a scream. A rather girlie scream, as he tumbles through the sand and falls through the air and space that wasn't under the lizard moments earlier. An empty void. He tumbles headfirst into the blackness.

Hackney looks up as a faint scream; then a dull thud echoes across the dunescape. It is Littleton's body making contact with the long-buried floor of a cavernous room, many feet below the surface. A rising dust cloud caused by his landing floats upward in the air. For a moment, Littleton lays still, staring skyward, his head resting on the hard, cold floor.

Gradually, breath returns to his lungs; he squints, dazed and stunned, realising that he has fallen some distance through the open cavity above him. Littleton raises himself to his feet and looks up, shielding his eyes to see Hackney staring down at him from about 25 feet above. The sunlight streams in around him as visibility returns, he can focus on the other occupants of the room that he now finds himself placed in.

Opening his eyes more fully, he is not alone; many faces smile back, hideously frozen grins, all around him in the semi-darkness. Some figures still clad in most of their mortal flesh, now dried hard and resin-like, shrunken to the bony armature beneath. Skeletons, dozens of them. Some were sitting, most lying in twisted shapes, in a macabre railway waiting room where there were no chairs.

Littleton's arrival at this, their last resting place had caused a fine cloud of dust to hang in the air. As it cleared, his surroundings were revealed in greater detail. The cloud settled, again to the floor, the air becoming frigid, stale, and still.

'Great Caesar's Ghost! Are you alright?' Littleton looks up at Hackney's silhouetted figure above him.
'There's a lot of dead people down here, Hackney,' he said matter-of-factly.
'Are you sure?'

'Believe me.'

'By jove, what do they look like?'

'Dead. I can see their bones; it's horrible. Could you go and get some help and some more people to get me out of here?'

'On it right away. Toodle-pip, I'll be back before you know it.' With these instructions, Hackney disappears from view.

Before Littleton can say anymore, he is gone. Littleton takes a seat on a small step and absentmindedly starts a noughts and crosses game with one of the skeletal mummies opposite, scribing on the dusty floor.

Twenty minutes passed slowly; he had won several games but lost a few more. No sign of Hackney and the others. Littleton feels his palms begin to moisten. He tries not to make socket contact with the nearest poor unfortunate that grins back at him, resting, against the painted peeling wall, dressed in the remnants of his old tattered robes and reed sandals.

Twenty minutes turned into an hour. The angle of light shafting into the room slowly changes and moves along the floor.

No Hackney.

The shaft is suddenly broken by the silhouette of a head and shoulders, turbaned and smiling. Littleton can make out the features of a young Arab boy maybe fourteen or fifteen years old.

A voice echoes down into the recess. 'Hello, mister.'
'Hello,' Littleton calls back.
'Do you want to sell one of those?'
Littleton, not initially understanding the question, looks around him.
'Do you want to sell one of those?" the voice repeated.
'One of what?" asks Littleton, craning his neck and shielding his eyes.
'The 'deadies'. Do you want to sell one or two?'
Littleton, now understanding, looks around at the 'deadies'. 'Do you mean these?' pointing at the dry mummified bodies. 'Yes, I can help you out if you give me two 'deadies', mister.' 'You mean you want two of the 'deadies' in exchange for my freedom?'
'Yes, I will pass down a rope, you can tie two of them on, and I will pull you up after.'
'Where is everyone else?' asks Littleton, beginning to lose his temper.
'Lunch then, siesta.' The voice replies in good but heavily accented English.

A heavy hemp rope drops to the chamber floor.

Littleton contemplates the exchange of two of the 'deadies' for his freedom. This young fellow was a pint-sized unscrupulous rogue, but Littleton, tired of the confines of the dark chamber, takes two of the nearest hard brown-skinned skeletons and binds the rope around their waists.

He shouts to the young turbaned villain to pull them skyward. They begin to rise above the floor like players in a macabre acrobatic circus act. Disappearing through the hole that Littleton created when he fell through to arrive in his present predicament. The two stiff figures disappear through the opening. Five minutes pass, and nothing happens.

Hackney's face then reappears, a little out of breath but a welcome sight nonetheless.

'Where in heaven's name have you been?' Littleton gasps.
'Sorry, I got waylaid over lunch. Who were the three skinny guys running like the blazes from here? I tried to catch them, but they were too fast for me, I'm afraid.'
Littleton begins to answer, but then, too exasperated, he replies

For the second time that day, a rope drops from the opening above. This time, Littleton is able to fasten it around his waist and soon is surface-bound. Once above ground, hot and sweaty, it dawns on him that he has indeed discovered something. The excitement begins to well within. Just a flutter at first, then building into a steam train of unbridled jubilance.

'Hackney, old chum, I think we have discovered something!'

Men are brought to clear the area around the hole. After which steps are revealed leading down to the chamber, which was sealed from above, entombing the present unfortunate inhabitants over two thousand years ago. The other areas of the dig are amalgamated and all excavation is focused on Littleton's hole.

Elizabeth is ecstatic; the day is spent enlarging the access to the chamber and examining the contents. The bodies inside were deemed to be workers and labourers of antiquity. Sealed with their secret forever in the darkness until now. The day passes quickly, and just before the evening begins to descend, the name of Asanti is made out on an old breadboard and biscuit tin brought from the room's recesses. The sweeping excitement was contagious, and the camp was in excited chatter. No one fought for the first hour; only a few desert rodents died. Hackney was to record that day in his diary thus...

'Cor blimey, would you believe it? We have found something. Something big. I am eating soup. Alas, I cannot forget Sonia Sinclair. If possible, I would rescue and rehabilitate her. I will close now as someone is knocking on our tent flap.'
'Did you hear that, Hackney? Someone is knocking on our tent again. See who it is, will you? No more congratulations please, I'm very tired.'

Hackney drew back the tent flap, to see a gentleman standing before him not dissimilar in appearance from himself. Moustached and quizzical.

'How do you do? Permit me to introduce myself,' lifting his hat and handing Hackney his card. He, too, is English, and his accent belies an expensive education. A scream echoed across the camp. Littleton stands up and joins Hackney and the new arrival. Looking past him and over his shoulder at a minor scuffle that had broken out over dinner, over tents, and over anyone who wasn't fighting.

'Good grief, what is the matter with this lot? Can't an explorer and his successful archaeologist get any peace?'

Looking towards the stranger at his tent door, Littleton eyes the character with a very mistrusting glare.

'What can we do for you, Sir?' Littleton asks rather brusquely.
'Well, we heard of your discovery from across the valley, and if I can be of any assistance, I would be delighted to lend a hand in any way I can?' The soft-spoken stranger stands back and awaits the reply of his fellow countryman.

This competition and a fellow kinship of like-minded camaraderie are about to be broken.

'Oh, I see. Do you want some of the glory? We do all the work and pinpoint the very spot, and you show up for dinner?' The gentleman is quickly taken aback by Littleton's tone and reaction to his offer of help.

'I merely meant I have men and resources from my benefactor, Lord Carnarvon. Sir, I can assure you that I have searched many seasons for a very different quarry. We are looking in the next valley over for The Boy King.'

Littleton throws his head back in mock disgust, 'Tut, is that the best you can come up with, Tut?'
'How did you know? We have been searching under a veil of complete secrecy?'

'Listen, mate; you can go and find your own tomb; we are handling this without any nosey parker from across the next valley. Go on, be off with you; I'll set the chickens loose. Bloody cheek.'

The fellow turns dumbfounded and highly insulted - now irritated by the extreme of Littleton's reaction to the offer of his help.

'And don't come back!' Littleton shouts to the disappearing figure as he makes his way through the tent village.
'Can you imagine that, Hackney? Bloody cheek, we do all the work, then he turns up-after a piece of the glory.'
'Who was he?' Pointing to the card Hackney is still holding.

Hackney lifts the card and lowers his spectacles to read it. He holds the square card up to the oil lamp to get more light.

'HOWARD CARTER, Archaeologist. He's got some rather fancy letters on his card and letters after his name.'

'Never heard of him. A loser, the only thing he will ever discover is sand,' Littleton scoffs. The two men giggle in the luminosity of the oil lamp's glow.

Chapter Thirteen

It's a Cracker!

Vasak has a wide, beaming smile on his ten-year-old face. His clear olive complexion radiates with excitement. He has made more money today than any day he has known before in his short life, and all for reporting to Sergeant Koresh the unimportant facts of the present excavations going on in 'The Valley Where Everyone is Buried'. Five shillings was a tidy sum.

The nearest wire station was a few miles away, but the hot walk between the dunes, skipping between the cart tracks, was worth it. His dirty, sandaled feet practically hopped all the way. This and the money he got from the sale of the 'deadies' from the stupid foreigner in the hole will go towards a pineapple, maybe two?

Sergeant Koresh paid young Vasak as he read the note paper and the telegrapher's pencil scribbled words. Smiling to himself as he unconsciously adjusted his underwear, that desert sand can get awfully scratchy. He had been pretty damned clever to notify all the surrounding villages that the reward was available for any information regarding the Fern expedition. He would make plans that would put an end to the run of good fortune the foreigners were currently experiencing. In reality, he needn't bother as both Littleton and Hackney were quite capable of doing it themselves and were thus so engaged at this very moment.

The dawn light casts its warm glow several miles away upon the excited encampment. Breakfast is brought from the hotel kitchen on carts pulled by pale white oxen. Moppity Saunders kept the inmates from the asylum in an ordered, consecutively numbered line as they collected their grapefruits and bread. Talk is exclusively about the prospect of today's search.

Elizabeth Fern has already begun to catalogue everything that has been cleared from the first room after yesterday's discovery. Farouk had found himself a working camera and was recording everything by the silver plate technique, revealing himself as something of a talent in that area. His impromptu work was of an astounding quality and definition, to say nothing of his artistic composition. All this was done from his makeshift darkroom tent.

At the far end of the now empty room that was cleared and ready for further excavation is an opening that leads to many corridors that, on their initial inspection, seem to extend beneath half of the immediate terrain, stretching for hundreds of yards. A labyrinth of corridors and tunnels. The manpower and time to search them was going to be considerable. It is at this small opening that Littleton and Hackney now stare; both saying nothing while consuming their grapefruit and bread.

'I know we agreed to wait until Elizabeth was organised and ready, but why don't we light a torch and take a quick look? What harm can it do?' says Littleton. Hackney nods, smiling mischievously in agreement.

The two now would-be explorers and unlikely archaeologists enter the darkness with pounding hearts and lighted torches. Their imagination is filled with images of ancient riches and jewel-adorned golden treasures that surely must be buried alongside the Chantress of Asanti. Many forms and likenesses could be seen rendered on every surface as they pass.

Illuminated by the glow of the torches were depictions of her legendary cracker collection. The most sought-after crackers of the ancient kingdom and second dynasty. Some of the corridors ended abruptly after what seemed like miles of meandering empty chambers.

Littleton slowly walks the wall, wondering at the drawings and figures. His torch burning in one hand and his small wooden-handled trowel in the other. Gently knocking the implement against the ancient plaster, listening for voids and anything that gives a hollow sound. At the corner of one chamber, they come across a step and the faint but visible sealed outline of a door. It looks to both men a promising sign.

'A door long since sealed,' Littleton whispers. 'What did you say?'
'I said, a door long since sealed.'
'Why are you whispering? There is no one else down here who can hear us.'

They both break into an uneasy laugh. Frantically, the two of them knock a hole just big enough to peer through into the room on the other side. The air that has not been breathed for centuries gently escapes its bounds with a slight hiss.

'Do you smell that, Hackney?' Taking a deep breath and urging Hackney to do the same.
'Phew, I say... it's quite strong, smells like cabbages, doesn't it?'
Littleton puts his torch through the hole they have created, he can now press an eyeball up to view what is beyond.

'Can you see anything?' Hackney asks impatiently.

'I can see many wonderful things.'

'Let me see.' Hackney is eager to view the treasure Littleton is describing.

265

Hackney scrambles and jostles Littleton out of the way. In his haste to knock Littleton from the viewpoint, his jostling causes his friend to release his grip on the burning torch that falls to the floor now on the other side of the wall. The two men get an eye to the opening and peer into the newly discovered chamber as the torch rolls along the floor and illuminates beautiful golden statues, ornaments, chariots, magnificent finery, and bejewelled surfaces glitter the array of many ancient objects cast flickering shadows around the walls, unseen for centuries.

'Amazing, incredible.'
'Odds bodkins,' Hackney exclaims.

The two men have, at this time, discovered treasure, a golden treasure beyond their wildest dreams. They are both breathless and can only marvel, gobsmacked at the ocean of ancient beauty before them. All of which seems to grow brighter by the minute. Their focus changes from the abundant richness before them to the source of the brightening illumination. It was no longer just the torch that provided them with light; now, a reed mat was burning quite brightly. The open-eyed wonderment is wiped from their faces; to be replaced by subdued terror as the flames begin to lick around the many objects, each being quickly consumed by the now-spreading inferno.

Five minutes pass like an hour as the two men frantically dig to try and get through the plaster wall to put out the fire. When it is suitably demolished, dripping with sweat, they are able to squeeze through the opening they have created. The fire is almost out, but to their horror and utter devastation in such a short period of time, almost nothing of the wondrous, ancient artefacts remains. The golden ornaments, were now just oddly shaped blobs of twisted blackened metal. Ashes where gold-leafed statues stood. The tunnels had acted like a chimney, keeping the smoke high above their heads but also fueling the flames with the oxygen they needed to become the short-lived inferno.

Standing amongst the rubble and smouldering ornaments that were to have made their names household words. They cannot help but feel a little saddened and disappointed. Littleton's nasal tick echoes around the chamber as he looks over the ashes at the devastation they have caused. It is several moments before they move or speak. With a sigh, they make their way back along the corridors, crestfallen and knowing they must break the news to the others. Emerging into the light, they are greeted by questions.

'Did you see anything down there; did you find anything? We wondered where you were?' The crowd are full of questions, eager to know more.

'Not really, some bits and bobs, stuff like that. A small fire and things, you know?' Littleton does his best to make light of the incident.

'What do you mean by a small fire?' Says one member of the crowd.

'A small fire, as I said,' Littleton answers the curious members of the growing crowd. 'Well, a big fire really, an accident with a torch. We will clean up the mess; we just need some buckets and brushes. Good as new, then. Carry on searching in your own sections!'

They troop on through the huddle of expectant reporters and villagers, returning moments later with buckets, brushes, and assorted cleaning equipment.

'Shall we come down and help with your section?' Another member of the dig asks.

'No, No, G-section can manage just fine - we'll clean up and carry on ourselves.'

The two men head off down into the chamber again.

'We were never cut out for this sort of work, Hackney. I'm beginning to think Jameson's summarisation of us is a lot closer to the truth than we care to admit.'

Both men stare at the charred, smouldering items with an air of despondency.

'What if there really is a curse, and the curse is that when you find the treasure, you accidentally will set fire to it?' muses Hackney.
'Bit of an odd curse if it is,' Littleton frowns.

Hackney nods absentmindedly, his mind elsewhere as he contemplates a way forward.

'What if there are more rooms like this one?' 'Another?'
'We never saw a mummy or casket or the like and presumably, she's in there somewhere.'
'I suppose that there could be another room? I mean, she was head chantress; she may have had a spare,' says Hackney.

Littleton's enthusiasm is starting to wane with each successive setback, but Hackney's words spark a little 'pep' back into him.

'Let's look for clues. The same way as we found the first, let's knock on the walls and try and perhaps make sense of these hieroglyphics,' he points to the frieze of figures and symbols running along the wall.
'I suppose we can try it once we have cleared up the mess we made of this one.'

Littleton, enthused, is now up for the task, staring at the walls.

'I had always thought of myself as something of a natural at deciphering these hieroglyphics things.' Littleton studies the figures.

'Hackney old chum, I know we have had a few setbacks; sometimes it's hard to keep a stiff upper lip, even though we are British and all that. But you are right, never give in, never surrender.' He stares at the painted murals on the wall. 'I am, some might say, something of an expert in the field of intuition. I just need to use every ounce of my know-how?'

'Oh yes, I do remember your intuition,' Hackney replies, not looking all too convinced.

'We don't want to stumble into a trap; those Egyptians were sneaky devils, what with all that mummification and what not...'

'Quite,' Hackney nods.

'Forewarned is forearmed; if there is a curse, then we must be cautious.'

'Dash it, I don't know why I ever doubt you. You are a clever fellow, Littleton; I hadn't thought of that.'

Littleton is once more up for the task.

'So, let's see... ' he leans forward, retrieving a set of Pince Nez spectacles from his pocket and placing them on his nose. Studying the ancient painted stone inscriptions for a moment.

So, this is a squirrel-headed man next to a large budgie.'
'I think that's a falcon and a jackal, old man,' Hackney corrects him.

Littleton squints and mumbles to himself in deep thought as he moves closer to the wall.

'They seem to be standing on a large banana,' he finally exclaims.
'I think that's a reed boat,' Hackney replies. 'Stop interrupting Hackney.'
'What I would say this all means... is... that you should not step on a banana when a budgie is near your jackal; yes, I think I'm right; it's a warning the banana is the same shape as the moon it's telling us something, Hackney.'
'By jove. What do you reckon it is Littleton?'
'I haven't the faintest notion...' he sighs.

As fate would have it, after several minutes of knocking their trowels against the walls, it is Hackney who comes across the slight hollow sound. At the far end of the chamber, painted on the wall and sculpted in relief, are the figures of deities at a ceremony.

Hackney smudges away some of the freshly deposited soot

from the recent fire and holds his torch closer. 'It is the Chantress look.' He points to the central figure in the relief. A seated figure in robes holding what appears to be a tin of biscuits. Surrounded by plates of crackers and preserves, probably Nile jam.

Littleton smiles and uses the wooden handle end of his trowel to knock more firmly on the wall so that he might hear the hollow sound of another room beyond this one. The dampness and sudden shock of his more severe knocking have an adverse effect on the wall's carved and painted reliefs.

Before their eyes, the figures painted so realistically centuries before begin to sag, the plaster releasing its tenuous grip upon the surface of the wall, and the artwork from the age of antiquities slides gracefully to the floor like a brittle fabric to become just another pile of rubble. A colourful jigsaw of pieces. It left a stark plain surface to which it had been adorned and attached.

'Oh, crikey, I must have tapped it a little harder than I intended.'

The removal of the plaster, all of it unintentionally, now exposed the faint but discernible outline of another sealed door. (Yes, another strange and coincidental anomaly.)

'We must get help,' Hackney gasps with a smile of anticipation.

This time, Littleton and Hackney deem it prudent to return along the corridors and enlist the help of others rather than go it alone, a wise decision.

The professor and his daughter are brought. Several of the more experienced diggers start to excavate the new door. Safely illuminated this time by electric lamps from a battery bank and powered by a paraffin-fueled generator. The debris from the wall is gingerly removed, as many faces peer into the blackness that is the newly discovered second room. Its contents appear slowly before them like the deck of a ghost ship at dawn.

Moppity Saunders keeps the asylum helpers in an ordered line as they pass out the baskets of rubble while reciting a slow mumble of a spirited song, something like an old sea shanty with indiscernible lyrics - with the exception of the word 'willy' that is repeated too many times. It keeps them smiling and their spirits up as it is hot, gruelling work.

The cables that lead to the electric lights have been rigged to wooden posts with electricity from the generator that runs above ground. The professor increased the voltage with a turn-dial wooden handle on a transformer and the brightness was increased to the strings of the bare incandescent light bulbs. In the brightness, the newly discovered room's contents became more discernible; many wonderful carved and gilded objects surrounded a large central piece.

The largest and most unusual artefact, which was not hard to miss behind the excavated wall, was a mysterious and almost perfectly round object. Shaped like a giant coin with a flat roughly textured surface, it rested on trestle legs supported by a gilded ceremonial table. Everyone stared at the vision. This object was rumoured and until now thought to be just the stuff of legend. The Ancient Egyptian Ritual Burial Biscuit. It was round and it was huge.

A hush settles over the excavation.

'I thought I'd never see one. The cracker was to sustain the Chantress on the journey to the afterlife and beyond. The centuries-hardened surface, acting like a huge coffin or casket.' Moppity is as pleased as her father.
'It's incredible,' the professor whispers in hushed tones.
'Wonderful,' says Hackney, taking his cue from everyone else.

 'It's a big Cracker,' exclaimed Littleton, stating the obvious to everyone.

'Indeed, it is,' smiles the professor.

The Burial Biscuit of Asanti. The cracker that would sustain her on her journey into the afterlife.'

When all the rubble was cleared, people stared at the unexpected sight they had unearthed. A giant biscuit cracker maybe ten feet in diameter and perfectly formed as if fresh from a gigantic shop-bought packet.

'Gentleman, I believe we are looking at the largest ceremonial burial cracker ever found,' Professor Saunders speaks gleefully. 'The largest ritual burial biscuit ever to be unearthed in any of the tombs, until the present day.'
'You what?' says Littleton, staring hard at the large biscuit before them.
'Well, I say... it's quite a bobby-dazzler alright, eh, Littleton?' exclaimed Hackney.
'I've only come across one such example before, and that was a long time ago; I forget where or when or how it was ... now... what was I saying?'
'She's in there, is she?' Littleton asks.
'She is,' the professor cannot avert his admiring gaze from their discovery.
'We came all this way and did all this work, and all we find is a giant cracker?'

Littleton is slightly disappointed, despite the professor's growing enthusiasm as he continues.

'Dating back to the dawn of antiquity the ancient ritual of the dynasty of Palperri, which means 'people of the biscuit, clan of the cracker' followers of the crusty loaf made these crackers. It was customary to embalm and preserve the revered and exalted ones' remains, not within the standard procedures of the time.

Instead, the substance that was usually used to dry the body, Natron, was replaced by special ingredients known only to the temple's high priests. These ingredients were bought and mixed in great quantities, the body was then placed within the mix, and the whole lot was fashioned to replicate the most popular ceremonial cracker or biscuit of the day. In this case, whole Egyptian long grain with Byzantine Sesame is not dissimilar to a very popular line at my factory now that I remember. It was called the Khari Cracker awfully good with an aged stilton and a fine port. Ah, those were the days, my friends; I thought they'd never end. We'd sing and dance forever and a day... '

'Father, you are slipping again. Don't let your excitement get the better of you; what else can you tell us about the cracker?'

The professor's daughter, Moppity, interrupts with a sense of urgency in her voice, aiming to keep the professor on track.

'What cracker?' the professor smiles as he again notices the biscuit he has been talking about, he almost loses his tack, but his delicate mental footing grasps, then gingerly regains its grip.

'Yes, yes, the symbolic food in abundance for journeying to the afterlife. The nature of the ingredients used to preserve the body and the hardened surface of the cracker, or as I said, burial biscuit, when dry, acting like a sturdy coffin or sarcophagus.'

He taps the surface hard with his knuckles, bending down to take a closer look, frowning and rubbing his stubbled chin.

'Someone or something has been at this cracker.' People gasp, fearing the worst.
'Tomb robbers?' several voices ask.
'No, something far worse to make it unpalatable for robbers and humans, a secret ingredient was added: Horrock, a foul-tasting hallucinogenic poison that drives men insane, but unfortunately, Horrock is absolutely delicious to the Karap Beetle. And this cracker is infested with them.'
'The Krap beetle?' says Littleton as he gazes across the surface of the cracker.
'That's right, it's pronounced 'K-a-r-a-p' Beetle, Karap, a close relative to the Scarab. It's pronounced the same as the stinky stuff that comes out of the wrong end of a camel.'

Elizabeth frowns.

The giant biscuit is rolled slowly along the corridors. After many centuries, it is surprisingly robust. Eight men are needed to move it carefully up the steps to the cleared space and the next chamber. A large platform-supported trestle table has been set up beneath a taught stretched canopy to shield the excited proceedings from the intense rays of the relentless desert sun. Every inch of the cracker needs to be delicately and finely examined with meticulous care.

It is indeed a huge biscuit from the past and its sight has a mesmerising effect on those close by as it is rolled across the almost level terrain. It is at this point that the unthinkable happens. A lone bearded worker, who has had one too many Yaca at lunchtime, suddenly becomes startled by a small brown Darwin toad that he swears was wearing a little yellow turban and sunning itself on its back, it being a bad omen to see such a sight on a Tuesday at the time of unearthing an ancient relic.

Today was a Tuesday.

Panic spread throughout the camp and affected the rest of the workers like wildfire. In the upset and confusion, the biscuit is released and slowly begins to roll unguided down the hillside, gradually picking up speed and bouncing higher with each successive contact with the rockier terrain and hardened road surface further down. The amazed crowd could only watch as the huge biscuit bounced out of control and then out of sight.

'Wow!' Several inmates shout as it rolls past them. Others shout, 'Ulla Ulla!' (which means wow in the local dialect). The integrity of the ancient cracker held up surprisingly well. 'Did you see that?' is the open-mouthed question posed by an astonished Hackney.

The professor had, in a vain attempt to stop the rolling relic, left the ground with a spirited leap and clung to the surface of the rolling biscuit as best he could, somehow finding purchase enough to maintain his grip. Now, biscuit and Professor Saunders were cart-wheeling down the mountainside. It was as if the whole scene was some fanciful tale from a far-fetched fantasy. But it is all too real!

For a moment, there is silence, then a few men set off after the professor and the cracker. Littleton and Hackney included. After cresting the first ridge, the bouncing path of the out-of-control rolling relic can be seen as it smashes its way along its given course down the incline. It has taken just a few moments to cover quite a distance, and it is discerned that it must have been heading for the lower road leading into the town of Bolloxi. The road on which a certain police convoy had been proceeding with Sergeant Koresh at its head. Travelling in the front car with three of his villainous cronies. He had evil on his mind. He would pay these fools back for thinking they had outwitted him.

But the last thing Koresh was to see that day was the giant biscuit-cracker bouncing towards them. Unpalatable and unstoppable, with Professor Saunders clinging desperately to the side of the ancient artefact.

The flying biscuit hit the car dead centre from above, instantly annihilating the occupants with a sickening crispy crash. Then, it came to rest in a thousand pieces smashed on the surrounding rocks, a mess of old car wreckage, new body parts, old crumbly body parts, cracker, and Koresh. 'By-crikey!' Hackney gasps. 'Where did the professor go?'

'I think he was flung off before the impact,' someone shouts. 'Ulla, Ulla,' a few others gasp.

As the small crowd looks toward the devastation of the road below, a loud explosion booms across the desert sand from the head of 'The Valley Where Everyone is Buried.' A fireball erupts behind their backs at the entrance to the tomb, and the surrounding encampment is thrown into disarray. Everyone spins around, and some begin to head back up the hillside toward the source of the blast. Others look for the professor.

It's turning into a busy day!

The group that had headed back to the camp arrived at the blast site and caught their breath. It is discerned that Farouk's chemicals, in his makeshift darkroom, had been a trifle more volatile than he had been given cause to believe. The tent and adjacent larger storage tent containing all the articles that had yet to be retrieved were no longer where they had been. The fumes from the large hydrochloric acid jars have been left to mingle with the ammonia nitrates and the results were extremely volatile.

Farouk, slightly dazed at the ferocity of the explosion, and the resulting fireball, lifts himself from the sand. The fireball looks to have consumed all other evidence that they had ever found anything here at all; in 'The Valley Where Everyone is Buried' today, it looks like a blast site.

The only items that survived and could be retrieved were a royal cheese knife and a matching breadboard, that miraculously had avoided the flames; both lay on the ground in a pathetic reminder of the Hall of Treasures beyond imagination.

Elizabeth knew nothing of the calamitous action at the camp. Earlier that morning, she had taken a camel into Bolloxi to wire Lord Fern of the unfolding progress of the successful expedition, and to notify him of the wondrous discoveries of the Tomb and its contents that they were about to open.

The Chantress had finally been found.

All successfully found in Lord Fern's name, a crowning glory to his archaeological career. Thankfully, she was not yet aware of the calamities that had taken place back at the camp; her ignorance, however, was short-lived as the plume of dark smoke arose like an ominous mushroom of impending burnt antiquities from behind the crest of the hillside. She used a little more riding crop on her camel than usual as she headed back up the hillside.

'We'd better save the cheese knife and board. It'll remind us of this time as explorers and discoveries of great treasure. You take the knife; I'll take the board,' says Littleton.
'We may as well start packing.' Hackney turns to watch the troop of helpers and diggers filing down the mountain.

Hackney comforts Moppity Saunders and offers to find the professor's mortal remains as Elizabeth and the camel appear, racing up the track toward them at a considerable speed. As she draws closer, she begins to assess the damage.

'What the fuck!' She shouts at the top of her voice.
'We have had a bit of an accident. Oh well... ' Littleton sniffs, 'I think it may be time for us to go home.'

Chapter Fourteen
Culmination Confrontation

The gleaming Pullman draws into Victoria Station, the proceeding engine billowing clouds of steam, swathing the jubilant crowd on the platform in white misty ghosts. A uniformed band strikes up the brass section, and the reception of assembled committee members straightens their hats and ties. Banners and colourful taffeta paper decorations are strung along the platform from pillar to post. It is almost dark now; the early evening glow of the gas lights cast long shadows on the attendant throng of well-wishers and dignitaries on the spotlessly clean, swept platform floor.

Littleton and then Hackney peer out of the carriage window, both aware that the story that Elizabeth has concocted differs fundamentally from the truth, in as much as the expedition was a complete and abject failure, not the resounding success that she has spoken to her beloved father about. Not the success that W. J. Jameson has been publishing for months in 'A History Weekly.'

Certainly not the landmark in archaeological achievement that they had hoped it would be. In short, all this pomp and ceremony was not warranted.

The expectant crowd awaited glorious treasures and tales of discovery. Not the reality that both men knew to be true. As the boiler was dampened and the brakes squealed the iron wheels to a halt, one of the faces in the crowd stood out amongst the smiles of others. A cold face with bony skull-like features and small black eyes filled with the stare of an evil disposition.

Smiling, Singleton Sinclair raised his hat slightly as he saw his quarry. The two men gulp. In the time they had been away, the vision of Sinclair had not faded from their thoughts. His eyes had lost none of their piercing coal blackness.

'Did you see who that was? Why is he here? Why would he come and meet us? Wait until he finds out about his daughter; he's going to be pretty mad.'
'Perhaps he already knows; that's why he's here,' Hackney winces.

A slight sweat begins to dampen Littleton's brow. 'He probably hopes to get his hands on the fictitious casket that Elizabeth has invented...'

As the two men step, waving half-heartedly from the train, a couple of burly officials march forward, both heavily built, sporting officious-looking railway uniforms.

'Excuse me, sirs, but there is some official paperwork and disembarkation formalities to go through before the ceremony. If both you and Mr. Hackney step this way, we can have them dealt with in a moment.'
'By all means, gentleman, lead the way,' says Littleton.

They jostle their way through the cheering crowd, shaking a few hands and receiving a few more pats on the back. The officials lead them into a quiet waiting room and up some stairs through a hallway into a large office above a freight storage warehouse. The coolness and silence, a welcome respite from the near hysteria going on outside. Not noticing that the officials cover any retreat, the two men are led into a small annexe, unaware of any consistency in the uniformed men's story.

The door closes loudly behind them, but it is the vision before them that has them worried. Behind a large desk sits a man they know not to be any official of the railway's bureaucracy. It is the bony, cold smile of Singleton Sinclair that comes from behind tented fingers.

Littleton and Hackney make for the door, only to find it blocked by the two bogus officials, who, it would appear, are, in actuality, Sinclair's hired goons.

'Gentlemen, we meet again; how nice it is to see you so well. Who would have thought that you would accomplish your task, not I? I'm sure not even yourselves.' Both men know they are trapped. 'At least this place is quiet from the railway noise, it's where I do my business. This evening, my business is you two.' He pauses a moment…

'Have I told you why I use the signature of the Black Scarab?'

Both men look at each other and then nod at Sinclair. 'It's because of your hairy legs, isn't it?'
'Precisely, now let's get down to business, that casket of yours I mean to open it, as by rights it's mine.'

Again, the two men exchange a worried glance. Littleton tries to explain.

'Oh, the casket, yes, well, really, that's a bit of a mistake as well... well, not a mistake, more of a mix-up really, as there is no casket to speak of. So, I guess you could say it is a rather sorry tale. It was a story to keep everyone happy; we didn't actually find one. We didn't find anything but a... you're going to find this funny, a giant biscuit, a huge ceremonial cracker, and unfortunately that got smashed to pieces down a desert road that was... ' Littleton warbles. Hackney nods.

'Shut up! Your childish gibberish already makes me tired and somewhat angry. You'd better start telling me the truth if you want to see the outside of this room.'

He pauses and distractedly fondles a small, black, jade fetish between his bony fingers. A beetle. He stands and draws himself up, leaving the desk and walking beside Littleton.

'And do you know what's happened to my daughter?' 'Ha, I'm glad you asked that.'

'No,' says Hackney, quickly closing down any incriminating confession that may have been forthcoming from Littleton.

'You do know you are not going to see the outside of this room, don't you?'

'We are not?' whimpers Littleton.

'Talking of caskets though your fate is rather ironic, as is the nature of my revenge. I'm going to make you two like the gods of Egypt... immortal.'

'Immortal?' Again, Littleton's lips murmur in concern.

'Not in the strict sense of the word, but you will live on forever in people's minds and be gazed upon by the common man for many years to come.'

Hackney frowns at Littleton, then casts his eye over Singleton for a clue.

'What do you mean, Sinclair?'

Sinclair grabs Littleton's wrist, holding it awkwardly as he speaks.

'You two are going to join the leagues of the dead within my very own collection.' Singleton Sinclair starts to laugh, his excitement getting the better of him, his breath coming in short gulps and quickening to a steady pant. 'You're going on a trip to the museum, alright, and you won't be coming back!'

He lets go of Littleton's wrist, which he had been gripping so tightly. Littleton stares at the red marks that Singleton's bony fingers have left on it.

'The two of you are going to become star attractions at exhibits, such as royal exhibits. In an hour or so, you will be king and queen Rhatu Phatu, rulers of the lower regions.'

'Lower regions?' Hackney quizzes him with a puzzled look across his face.

'With the aid of several hundred feet of ancient bandages, you will experience all the joys of mummification, as our beloved Egyptian royalty so enjoyed it.'

'What?' Hackney is having a hard time with Sinclair's explanation.

'You will be bound and suffocated by the very bandages that they were buried in thousands of years ago, then sealed in the genuine, painted sarcophagus.'

'I say, Sinclair, that's a frightfully bad show.'

Sinclair just laughs... 'Ha, ha, ha, ha ...... Ha, yes ... it's not really cricket, is it, but then I've never been much of a team player.'

'You fiend!' both men exclaim in wide-eyed unison.

'Indeed, I am a fiend and a clever one to boot,' Sinclair snaps back.

The men are unsure if Sinclair means to carry out his devilishly fiendish plot.

'I knew we'd find a use for all those bandages; we unwrap so many mummies here and powder each of them along with anything else handy. Good for whatever ails you, and we've unwrapped quite a few this month,' he points to some grizzly, dark and hardly recognisable figures, dry dismembered body parts lying around the workshop.

'Luckily, we save all the bandages. It's like Christmas here, and we never throw away anything useful. We keep the wrappings; you never know when they'll come in handy.'

The two heavies, who had merely stood by the door until this point, took their cue from Singleton. The two captives' jackets were unceremoniously removed, and the two overwhelmed men struggled in the uneven contest, only to be thrown violently onto the debris-ridden tables.

'Of course, it will be a lot easier to turn you into ancient icons from the ancient kingdom if you don't struggle, so I've had the forethought to concoct a little something to put you to sleep, permanently. I don't expect you to drink it willingly, but just a little on your tongue should do the trick.'

Singleton picks up his cane and unscrews the silver chaliced top to produce a small delicate glass bottle containing a bile green liquid. Hackney watches him intently as the three men hold him fast. Two more of Singleton's men had entered the room from the side door, each equally as burly as the men holding onto Littleton. It looks like it's the end. Littleton, momentarily infused with vigour, starts to thrash, but to no avail; squirming and writhing, he has little hope of twisting free.

One of the hired goons, tired of Littleton's contortions, smacks him hard across the face, this action strangely has the effect of giving him the adrenaline shot he needs to keep up his eel impression with renewed effort. His new lick of energetic kicking and thrashing is quite a surprise to his captors. Sinclair approaches with a fiendish grin, as he holds the small glass tube slowly, unscrewing the silver top.

Littleton, with all his newfound strength, can do nothing but make one last lunge. Born of complete desperation, he kicks wildly in Singleton's direction, connecting with the old man's elbow and causing the deadly glass tube and its contents to spin into the air, spraying the light bile-like substance into the area between himself and the goons holding him. Littleton averts his head more out of tiredness than a conscious effort not to catch any fluid on his lips. The two thugs on each arm are not so lucky; each collects a few smattered drops across the face, including their lips.

'Don't taste it, wipe your mouth!' Sinclair shouts in surprise at the men, but it is too late; their grip weakens, and their vision becomes blurry as the poison starts to take effect on their tongues. Littleton pulls himself free. Sinclair clutches angrily at his bruised elbow. Hackney is still firmly in the grip of the two remaining thugs, and the other two lie at his feet, where they had fallen upon tasting the unknown concoction.

Seemingly unfazed by the setback, Singleton reaches into his waistcoat pocket and pulls out a small revolver, quickly regaining his smile and composure, back in control, he gestures with the gun. 'Right, you've only made things harder on yourselves. I'm going to let you know what it's like to be a live mummy. Pick up the bandages and begin wrapping yourselves now.'

Littleton and Hackney, after a moment's pause, feel compelled to do as he says; after all, he has the gun. They slowly start to wrap their limbs. When each man has wrapped his own arms and legs. Singleton orders them to wrap each other's torso and head until there is only a small slit for their eyes. This takes longer than expected, but after some time, they both become eerie bandaged figures, as instructed. Two live mummies from the past.

Sinclair begins to laugh loudly and contemplate his new creations, proud of his achievement and the execution of his idea. His hands begin to tremble, and his eyes blaze. Two open caskets lean against the far wall. The two caskets were to take the hapless reporters on a journey to the afterlife. Large and painted in the burial colours and likenesses of King and Queen Rhatu Phatu of ancient, central downtown Thebes by the gasworks. Each man is to take his place in the empty coffins.

There was a bit of an argument as to who should be the queen, but finally, it was settled and Littleton took his place as Queen Rhatu Phatu.

Once in position, the two men stare back at him, flanked on either side by the two remaining thugs; all three are struck by how realistic Littleton and Hackney now appear as 2000-year-old mummies.

'You know, I'm loathe to do this, but much as I'm delighted by the idea of a slow lingering suffocation. I'm going to have to dispatch you with a bullet. It's because of the noise, you see; we can't have you knocking on your coffins, can we now? So, it's at this point in the proceedings that we must say goodbye.' He lifts the revolver and aims at the first mummy, which begins to shake violently, it being Littleton beneath the bandages.

Suddenly, without warning, the lights go off.

Everything is in darkness; a shot echoes across the room, and then another ricochets off the many surfaces with a loud report.

'The lights! The lights! Get the lights!' Someone shouts in the darkness. The nearest thug races for the door as a struggle is heard in the blackness. Singleton unleashes three more shots in quick succession. As quickly as blackness had arrived, illumination returned to the windowless warehouse room. Now, only Sinclair and one-third of the criminal crew remained. A small trail of blood led away from the thug nearest the door.

Doubly shocking, though, for Sinclair was the disappearance of his planned latest exhibits, two wrapped mummies. The two heavy open sarcophagi are now empty. Singleton's eyes twitch as he surveys the two receptacles that were to have contained Littleton and Hackney's mortal remains. He scans around the room and laughs, only this time a little more nervously, as he weighs up his options.

Singleton addresses the general warehouse area, looking carefully for any movement. The many crates and artefacts prove excellent cover for the two hiding mummies. Hiding behind a large crated statue, out of view, sit such two mummies, the bandaged and shaking Littleton and Hackney.

Singleton moves slowly, gun in hand, toward the perceived hiding place; he moves around some of the strange ancient artefacts, expecting to find his quarry at every turn. There is an offbeat, wheeze-like tick that threatens to give them both away as Littleton does his best to control his persistent infirmity by holding his breath the best he can. Sinclair, meanwhile, comes across the bandaged, emotionless form of a darkened, rather tatty mummy in an open casket. The mummy's unseeing eyes stare at him. Singleton smiles and unloads two bullets into the mummy's chest. It doesn't flinch. The swathed reclined figure is the genuine article.

Frustrated, he looks around further.

'Gentleman!' he shouts. 'Let's do a deal? I'm sure we can come to a deal, show yourself!' Sinclair starts to look less than comfortable as he shouts again aloud. Littleton and Hackney watch from between the crates as a large figure appears from the darkness and cups both men's mouths - to stifle any screams.

'Farouk, thank heavens it's you, how did you know we were here?' they whisper.
'I followed you when the officials met you from the train. I smelt something fishy, and I don't mean Babylonian mackerel.'

'Good job then, it was your handiwork. All the light switch stuff saved our bacon,' Littleton speaks quietly.

'Listen, I will deal with the last big fellow; you will have to rush, Sinclair,' and with that, Farouk, like a trap door spider, retreats into the darkness behind him.
'What shall we do?' whispers Littleton to Hackney, the bandages starting to chaff and itch as they become very uncomfortable. They also had a rather noxious 2000-year-old smell.

'I have an idea; Sinclair has fired that revolver five times. I will cause him to fire it again, and then we rush him. It's a Webly 509 snub-nosed service revolver - they have a six-bullet magazine, he fired five.'
'Wow, that's very resourceful of you, Hackney.'
'I need to distract him; I have an idea,' Hackney says from beneath his bandages, taking hold of a slab of hieroglyphed stone on a nearby bench awaiting packing and shipping. Loosening his bandages, he pushes the stone slab between them to cover most of his chest, then arranges the wrappings so that it is not recognisable.

'What are you doing?' asks Littleton.

'This stone will act like a bulletproof vest. I get him to fire his last bullet at me, and then you rush him. Hopefully, he will also act as the distraction Farouk needs.'

With the stone shield now in place, Hackney slowly stands up and reveals himself to Sinclair, who faces him nervously. He is cautious of Hackney's easy vulnerability.

'One of you eh... where is your friend? I need to do a deal with both of you.'
'He's escaped and gone to get help, so you better give yourself up.'

Hackney bluffs as best he can with the dusty old bandages draped around his head.

'Then I'm afraid you will have to take his part of the deal,' raising his gun and taking aim as he levels the final bullet into Hackney. The shot hits Hackney squarely in the chest with a dull thud, as Hackney had hoped. A shot to the head may have had dire consequences. Hackney waited for his partner to jump Sinclair. He waited and waited. As Sinclair stands puzzled before frowning, he then begins to reload his revolver.

He places the fresh bullets in the chambers, and his confidence returns.

'Very clever, but let's see you shrug off this one,' he points the gun at a more acute angle, indicating a shot to the head. In his preoccupation with the standing mummy, the last goon has let his concentration lapse, and Farouk takes full advantage, jumping and bodily felling the fellow, there being a sizable weight difference between the two.

Sinclair spins around, only to have Littleton emerge from beneath a table and completely grip him around the waist. Farouk is momentarily shocked at the speed and recovery of his opponent; while Littleton's mummy struggles with a thrashing Sinclair, Hackney races over and grips the hand holding the revolver, smashing the knuckles hard onto the floor and knocking the pistol to the ground.

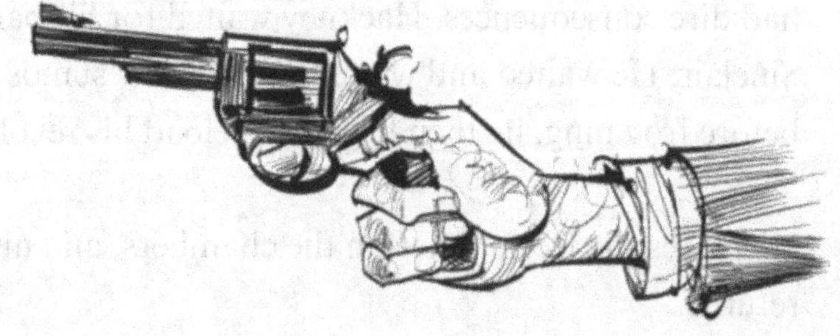

The two mummies grapple with Sinclair, and Farouk falls to the floor with the thrashing thug, both locked at each other's throats.

Singleton regains the gun as both mummies frantically hold onto Sinclair's hand, smashing the bony fingers repeatedly on the hard floor; again, the gun goes off. Singleton's rants and struggling subsides. The shot proves to be a particularly fortuitous one for Farouk, as the stray bullet finds its mark. The bullet caught the burly thug assailant that Farouk is fighting squarely between the eyes.

The two reluctant mummies lie on top of Sinclair, who is now snarling under their weight. The three men disentangle themselves, bandages and bodies and all, leaving Sinclair pale and gasping on the floor, looking very far removed from the stronger, sinewy villain of a few moments earlier.

Farouk rejoins Littleton and Hackney, and all three stare wide-eyed at Sinclair, who is now standing opposite. He becomes more aware that age is not on his side and feels a little guilty about the unequal struggle.

'It's my heart... my heart,' Singleton gasps.
'You seemed strong enough a moment ago,' Hackney says. The two men watch suspiciously as Sinclair rolls his eyes and gasps for breath.

'My pills, I need my pills, they are in my jacket pocket please... '

Farouk throws down the heavy trench-style coat that Singleton has been pointing at, and the garment falls across his prostrate body. Sinclair rummages quickly through its pockets. Then, smiling retrieves something nobody was expecting from inside its lining... another gun, now clasped firmly in his bony hand for the second time, only this time it's bigger than the last. Each man is more than disappointed at the advantage Sinclair has wrought so easily. They back away, hands above their heads, as Sinclair gets to his feet with renewed vigour.

'Didn't expect another gun, eh? Get over to the wall.'
The two mummies comply with Farouk and stand awaiting the inevitable.

'So, this is it?' Littleton stammers, 'Goodbye, Hackney, old chum.'

Singleton Sinclair's evil eyes flicker as he cocks the hammer to strike the firing pin and pulls the trigger, only to hear a loud click; his smile is immediately extinguished as he looks aghast at the malfunctioning weapon.

The three men facing the jammed revolver didn't need a second more. They all jumped head-first at Singleton, easily knocking him to the wooden floorboards. This time, they would not be taken in again by his wiley ways and sly shenanigans. Thrashing and kicking, the bony nemesis is manhandled into one of the open caskets, and the heavily carved lid is slammed shut.

Breathing heavily, Littleton half-manages a smile and starts to remove the loose bandages. Hackney does the same. They all feel a sense of relief that each has escaped with his life.

'It's a jolly good thing the gun jammed; we will call the police outside on the platform to deal with Sinclair; he'll be safe enough in here for now,' tapping the sarcophagus. He licks the blood from his split knuckles, and likewise, Hackney does the same, now free from his mummy's bandages, asks of no one in particular, 'I wonder if they have cherry cake and ginger beer?' 'I expect so, Hackney.'
Farouk smiles, 'You English with your sweet and savoury snacks; give me a bowl of glazed dates and some sugared Turkish delight.'
Hackney's ears perk up, 'I say, that sounds rather good.'

The band outside on the platform can be heard from inside the warehouse, the world, unaware of the deadly encounter that just a few moments ago had played out as they celebrated. The men make their way to join in the festivities.

The platform where the reception party is being held is in full swing, almost as if no one had noticed that the three men had been missing. They cheer the re-emergence of the three successful expedition heroes: the two feted explorers and archaeologists, Littleton and Hackney and Farouk!

'Hip, hip …Hooray!…Hip hip….'

****

This last monologue is narrated by the melodic tones of someone who sounds a lot like Sir Michael Horden, of Paddington Bear fame... his warm inflexions being perfect for such a monologue.

'The real success and achievements and, of course, failures of the Fern Expedition would wait to be told later, sometime later. But along with the Chantress of Asanti, not much is remembered in the history books today.

But for the rest of this day, all was ebullient and merry with congratulations and tales of daring-do smattering the many excited conversations. It would have been a shame to spoil the reception that had been held in honour of the two great explorers and discoverers of many ancient things, Mr Larry Littleton and Harry Hackney. So, they were to have their moment in the limelight, even their old boss, Wallace. W. Jameson, seemed pleased to have them back. The attendant crowd claps, the re-emergence from the railway offices of Littleton and Hackney, as they join the carnival-like proceedings.

The professor, having collected a broken ankle from his journey on the rolling burial biscuit, now sits in a similar position to Lord Fern, as both discussed the possibilities of a new dry snacks venture from the comfort of their respective wicker wheelchairs. Professor Saunders has committed some of the more elaborate crackers and biscuits to memory, along with an idea for something called the Bolloxi Biscuit. It was later to be Lord Ferns Biscuit Enterprises' most successful product.

But for now, the professor was convincing enough to talk his way right back into the business that still retained his name when he had been committed all those years ago. The knife and cheese board were presented to Lord Fern as at least some small token of the expedition.

Moppity Saunders talked with the two gentlemen about the possibility of opening a small Egyptian-themed public house come cabaret lounge, in London's Soho district. The Wandering Camel might not be an inappropriate name for such an establishment. Things were coming together nicely.

The most unlikely society wedding was announced that day between Lady Elizabeth Fern and one Lawrence Littleton. Lady Fern had orchestrated a fine courtship unperturbed by the reticence of her childhood sweetheart and his boyhood friends. Both Littleton and Hackney's involvement in the calamitous events that had led to the destruction by fire in the tomb, and the loss of the ceremonial burial biscuit, was soon forgotten.

In time, as was the Fern expedition, if you look, history holds very few references to it to this day. Just a few savoury recipes whose origins are obscure at best.

The idea of a cabaret lounge was shelved as, after a short engagement, Hackney was destined for a quieter, pastoral life, painting watercolours of hedgehogs and opening a small but successful sweetshop in the south of England, selling the family Fern product Saunders Crackers, alongside many aniseed-based confectionaries. His pretty wife-to-be was Mrs Moppity Hackney, formerly of Egypt, his now lovely betrothed and business partner in the venture.

Lastly, we must mention Singleton Sinclair, how could we not? The Black Scarab smuggling ring ceased all operations. The hemorrhaging flow of artefacts leaving the country diminished to a legitimate trickle. But, somehow, as fate would have it, part of Sinclair's fiendish plan, just as he had contrived, would go ahead. Not quite as he had wished. In as much as the closed sarcophagus with him in, it was collected and crated and shipped that same day before Littleton or Farouk had spoken to the station duty police. What with the celebrations, the heady pomp and circumstance of the afternoon and a severe mix-up in the paperwork at the docks, the unopened casket, with Singleton still in it, found itself on board a steamer bound for America.

It wasn't until the ship was halfway across the Atlantic that confusion and paperwork were cleared up, and Singleton, a little dehydrated but no worse for wear, appeared on the deck of the newly launched white star liner now on its maiden voyage. Cursing the salty air with words of vengeance and revenge, words that, of course, cannot be repeated here, as it blew over his bony features and spattered his drawn face with a biting cold, light rain.

A bitter, lone silhouetted figure, gripping the freshly painted handrail, standing above the huge gold letters on her bow, he vowed to get even upon his return to England. Again, fate, though would have a hand in his plans as is often the case, as those huge letters upon the prow above which he stood spelt out the name of the ship on which he now travelled... they spelt out the name RMS TITANIC.

The end
16th April
M.S

The Savoury Times - 'A fine wine with crisps of an adventure…'

The Cairo Cracker Chronicle - 'A rhubarb crumble of a tale- with custard!'

London HonkyTonk News - 'I'd say time well spent, like a buttered biscuit.'

Spider Gazette - 'I have hairy legs too.'

Crafty Crunchier & Biscuits Bazar - 'A fine recipe for a riveting caper just add imagination.'

Derek Rawlins Café - 'I like the words in this book.'

Sunday Sub Standard - 'It's a tale that's both savoury and sweet at the same time - like my Auntie Eileen.'

Wafers Weekly - 'One of the best books on the little-known Black Scarab affair that doesn't have a sausage in it!'

Mark Millicent
Author and Illustrator

Mark Millicent is a UK writer and illustrator. He works in the commercial advertising and film world. After thirty years abroad, he recently swapped LA and Southern California for the damper climes of the Welsh borders in the UK.

He can be found on Amazon and on the web at:

markmillicent.com

Let's be friends...

www.hbpublishinghouse.co.uk

hb_publishing_house

HB Publishing House

hb_publishing_house